Susanne O'Leary

Selling Dreams

Selling Dreams

Cover by JD Smith Design

ISBN-13: 978-1547189762
ISBN-10: 1547189762

Chapter 1

Chantal stretched out on the couch, the silk sheet cool against her bare skin. She propped herself on her elbow and gazed out of the window at the bay, where the early-morning sun was kissing the peaks of the mountains behind the Nice skyline. The azure water was calm with just a ripple or two near the shore, and the palm fronds barely stirred in the light breeze. It would be another hot day.

"Turn your head."

Chantal turned and looked at the man behind the easel. "Like this?"

"Yes." He held up a paintbrush and squinted at her. "I want you to put your hand down and stay supported like that on your arm."

"For how long? I'm getting stiff and I haven't had my coffee yet."

"I know, chérie, but try to stay like that for a few minutes at least. The light's perfect right now. It makes your skin glow and your eyes shine with exactly the same hue as the sheet you're lying on. Ice blue. I've never seen a woman with such eyes. With your black hair and that skin…" He kissed his fingers. "Sublime."

Chantal stifled a yawn. "Thank you. But please try to hurry up, mon amour. I have to go home and check on Jean and then go to the agency. We're very short-staffed at the moment, and the busiest season is just starting."

The man turned back to his work and added colour and light to the picture on the canvas, working silently.

"What are you painting?" Chantal asked.

"You."

"But what part of me?"

"I'm sliding the brush around your breasts."

She closed her eyes, imagining the light touch of the brush. "You're slipping down my waist to my hips," she murmured.

"Can you feel it?"

"Mmm."

"And now?"

"Oohhh," she whispered.

He glanced at her. "You must be psychic. Hold that expression. It's wonderful." He worked in silence for a few minutes and then put his brush and palette on the table beside the easel. "The light has changed. Enough for today."

Chantal stretched like a cat and rose from the couch, wrapping the sheet around her. "Can I see?"

"If you like. It's not finished yet."

"I know. But it'll give me an idea." She stepped around the easel, the sheet trailing behind her, and looked at the unfinished painting. The colours were breathtaking, with the ice blue of the sheet reflected in the woman's eyes and her skin like honey-coloured silk against the background of the view through the open window. The face was hers but without lines or expression, like that of a sphinx, looking into the distance or maybe even the future. Timeless. Ageless. Unrecognisable except for the eyes.

"You make me look young and old at the same time," she said.

He kissed her shoulder. "You are young."

She snorted. "Forty-nine is not young."

"You'll never be old to me."

She sighed and leant her head on his shoulder. "You're so good to me."

He put his arm around her. "You're my muse and my love. But I have to finish this painting before I leave. I have to go away for an assignment for a few days, and then I'll be back to prepare for the exhibition."

"And I have to go. I have several showings today. Thank goodness we're getting a new girl next week. It'll be such a great help."

"How is Jean?"

Chantal shrugged. "No better, no worse. The same."

"I'm sorry."

"Thank you. Not much to be done, really." She walked to the chair by the window and started to get dressed. "I'm so glad I can come here and be with you."

"Me too."

Chantal eased silk knickers over her hips. "Nobody knows what we do here. Or even that we know each other." She wriggled into her bra, slipped on a white cotton shift dress and pushed her feet into her sandals. "I really have to go." She walked back to him and kissed him on the lips. "À bientôt, mon amour. Don't forget to close the shutters and lock both the door and the gate."

"I won't."

She turned at the door, blew him a kiss and left him and her only source of happiness behind.

Chapter 2

It was dark when the plane landed in Nice. Flora looked out of the window but could see nothing but the floodlit tarmac, busy with trucks and personnel loading and unloading planes. The fronds of a dusty palm swayed in the breeze at the entrance of the terminal. She knew the airport was on the edge of the Mediterranean, but there wasn't even a glimpse of it. She gathered her bag and jacket and prepared to disembark. Tired and stiff, she stretched her back as she waited for the door of the plane to open so she could shuffle forward. The people behind her moved, pushing her into the man in front, making her step on his heel. He turned around to glare at her, and she met his irritated eyes with an apologetic shrug.

"Sorry," she said.

He didn't reply.

"I did it on purpose, of course," she said, attempting a cheeky smile. "I felt like annoying you. I was wondering how to attract your attention, and stepping on your foot seemed the perfect way."

He didn't smile back but looked friendlier. "Okay. Not your fault. Everyone's in a hurry to get off. Are you on holiday?" His barely discernible French accent gave his voice a charming lilt.

"No. I'm going to work here. If I get the job," she added wistfully.

He put his glasses on top of his head, where they nearly disappeared into his thick brown hair. "You're Irish?"

She laughed. "Yes. I suppose my accent gives me away."

"It's quite distinctive. I've just spent a week in Dublin and other parts of your country, so it sounds familiar."

"You were on holiday?" she enquired.

"No, it was for work." He peered along the queue of people ahead of him. "What's taking them so long?"

"I think they said the bridge wasn't working properly. But the doors are opening, I see, so we'll be getting off in a minute."

"If people can get their luggage down. Why do they have so much stuff?"

"No idea. I only have a small bag. I can't be bothered to lug all my belongings onto the plane."

The queue started to move forward. The man hitched his satchel onto his shoulder and fished out a card from the breast pocket of his blue shirt. "Here's my card. I live near Vence. It's a little town in the hills above Nice. If you happen to be touring around there, give me a call."

She took the card. "Thanks. I will—if I get the job. Otherwise I have to go back to Dublin straightaway."

"I hope you won't." They were nearly at the door of the aircraft.

"My name's Flora, by the way," she said, not wanting to lose his attention. "Flora McKenna."

He smiled, showing a dimple in his left cheek. "Well, bonne chance, Flora McKenna. I hope we meet again one day." Then he nodded at the crew standing by the door and disappeared into the crowd surging forward into the long corridor leading to the terminal.

Flora stuffed the card into the pocket of her linen jacket. Nice man. And very good-looking. But she would probably never meet him again. She left the plane with a feeling her trip had got off to a good start.

Half an hour later, Flora stepped into the dark soft night and breathed in the smell of petrol fumes mixed with the scent of flowers and pine needles—that special Provence smell she had read about. Above the din of traffic, she could hear a whirring chirping sound she assumed were the cicadas she knew were everywhere in this part of France. Being there was like a dream she never thought she would realise. She felt like pinching herself to make sure she wasn't asleep and would wake up in her dreary little flat in Dublin to start yet another day scouring the papers for a job. Finding the advertisement for the job in France and calling the number had felt like winning the lotto.

Things had happened so fast after Flora had called the number only a week earlier. A French estate agency was looking for Irish nationals with a good knowledge of French and some experience in the housing market. As the agency she was with in north Dublin had gone out of business, leaving her unemployed, she thought she would give it a shot. Her French was good, and she had a lot of experience selling houses in Dublin, which was possibly not the same as in France, but she was willing to learn. After a Skype conversation with the manager of the agency in Antibes, she was asked to book a flight so that they could meet in person. The job would be hers if she met all the criteria, whatever they were.

Flora took another deep breath of that magic air and felt the warm wind stirring her hair. It was time to go to the hotel by the airport, where she was to spend the night before she took the train to Antibes and the job interview. She could see the little shuttle bus with the hotel logo pulling up at the bus stop and lugged her suitcase to board it. Settling down on the seat for the short drive, she looked out at the street lined with palm trees and flowerbeds with roses in full bloom. This would have been magic were it not for that interview the next day. She tried to feel confident about it, but the thought that it would decide her future made her stomach lurch.

* * *

The train rattled along the coastline. Flora couldn't take her eyes off the sea and the blue skies, the beaches with colourful umbrellas and the sailing boats. The water was a deep sapphire blue, and she understood why this coast was called the Côte d'Azur by the French. There was no other blue like it. She didn't care that the train was so packed that she had to stand near the door, holding onto her suitcase with one hand and hanging onto the handrail for dear life with the other. The train swayed and bumped, jerking to a sudden stop at each station, where more passengers piled on, squashing into the already-cramped compartments. She wiped her forehead with the back of her hand and grabbed the handrail again as the train surged forward. The other passengers consisted mostly of tourists in shorts and T-shirts from countries all over the world. She could hear many different languages mingled with French spoken in the sing-song Midi accent.

It made her think of Madame du Jardin, her French teacher who was from Marseille. With her enthusiasm and support, she had inspired in Flora a love for France and all things French ever since her very first French lesson in the first year of secondary school. Madame du Jardin had sashayed into the classroom in her high heels, black pencil skirt and red silk blouse, breaking into a broad smile. She wore her black hair in a bun on top of her head, huge, hoop, gold earrings, and smelled of Shalimar by Guerlain. Flora was mesmerised.

From that moment, she wanted to *be* Madame du Jardin with her cheeky smile, flashing eyes and husky voice. Not that she ever succeeded, as her own strawberry-blonde hair, square jaw and strong bones were far removed from the Frenchwoman's petite frame and Latin looks. But Flora studied French as if her whole future depended on it, spent several summers in Paris, minding the spoilt children of the well-to-do and graduated with top marks. She always felt a little bit French, and looking out at the Mediterranean through the grimy window of the train, she felt a strong sense of belonging. She suddenly knew that even if she didn't get that job, she would look for something else. She would even mind children or clean hotel rooms as long as she could stay.

* * *

It didn't take Flora long to find the agency. Situated in the main street of Antibes, she could see the blue sign with *Agence du Soleil* in yellow letters over the entrance. She looked briefly at the photos in the window, advertising houses and apartments for sale and mentally gasped at the prices. Two hundred and fifty thousand euros for a studio of thirty square metres seemed very steep. And half a million for a two-roomed flat near one of the beaches? Real estate in this town was not very affordable. She pushed open the glass door, pulling her suitcase behind her, and nearly fell into the main office of the agency, where two women sat at computers behind a long counter. One of them looked up and tittered.

Embarrassed and flustered, Flora tried a smile. "Sorry. The door opened so suddenly and I had my suitcase so—"

The woman got up. "Sorry. We didn't mean to laugh. Are you okay?" Her cool tone didn't convey much sympathy.

"Yes. I'm fine. Just a little—you know—disoriented. I arrived in Nice last night, and then I took the train here this morning."

The woman nodded. "You must be the new girl." She held out her hand. "I'm Iris." She was pretty, with short dark hair, blue eyes and a smattering of freckles across her cute button nose. But there were lines around her eyes and mouth that hinted at late nights and something sad going on in her life.

Flora grasped her hand. "Flora McKenna."

"Are you joking?" Iris suddenly laughed.

Flora bristled. Why was her name so funny all of a sudden? "No, I'm not."

Iris calmed down. "Sorry. It's just that… She paused and tapped the other woman on the shoulder. "Take those earphones off, Daisy, and meet the new agent. Her name's Flora, would you believe."

The other girl took the earphones out of her ears and looked at Flora. "What?" Her eyes focused. "Flora? Oh my God, that's hilarious."

It suddenly dawned on Flora why Iris had laughed. Iris, Daisy and Flora suddenly seemed a ridiculous combination. "How strange," she said.

"Yes, quite odd," Iris said.

"Unusual name," Daisy said. "Kind of old-fashioned, isn't it?"

"It's because of Bonnie Prince Charlie," Flora explained.

Iris nodded. "That explains it. Flora MacDonald and the Isle of Skye and all that."

"That's right," Flora replied. "My mother read a novel based on that story before I was born, so I was named after Flora MacDonald."

"Who was she?" Daisy asked.

"A Scottish heroine. She helped this prince escape during the Jacobite risings in seventeen forty-six or something."

"Oh, okay. British history. Not something we get to learn in the good ol' US of A." Daisy smiled, shook her mop of light-blonde hair out of her eyes and held out her hand. "Hi, Flora, and welcome. As you heard, I'm Daisy. I'm from

New York, and Iris here is from London as you might have gathered from her posh accent. Where are you from?"

"Dublin," Flora replied and shook Daisy's hand.

"Daisy grinned. "Oh, great. I'm Irish too. My family name is Hennessy. It was good fortune that my granny was born in Cork, which meant I could apply for an Irish passport. This way I had no trouble getting a job in France." She turned back to the computer. "Anyway, Chantal will be back from her lunch break soon, so we'd better look as if we're working."

Iris snapped to attention. "You're right. She won't be too happy if we're caught chatting. In any case, I have to call that couple who wanted to see the house on the Cap. And get the cleaning lady to go in there and make the place smell nice."

"Tall order," Daisy muttered, her eyes on the screen. "The smell of drains in that place would knock down a horse."

"The owners should fix the drains," Iris said. "But they won't spend the money. So it's up to us to cover up the cracks until it's sold. I'll have to get some bread to put in the oven, too, for that home-baked smell. And lie about the roof."

"Lying. Worst part of this job," Daisy said. She peered at Flora. "Are you a good liar?"

"Um, not really," Flora had to admit.

"You'd better practice," Iris said. "Fibbing is a big part of this job."

"She's here," Daisy hissed as a tall thin woman with dark glossy hair and sunglasses pushed the door open.

Both girls turned to their computers and started tapping on the keyboards, while Flora stood in the middle of the floor, still holding on to her suitcase, looking at the woman who had just floated in the door, bringing with her the scent of expensive perfume and air of authority. She stopped and looked at Flora over the rim of her sunglasses. "Ah. Bonjour. Flora McKenna?"

"Oui, Madame," Flora whispered and managed to stop herself from curtseying. Those ice-blue eyes were scary.

"Bien. I'm Chantal Gardinier. Please come into my office. I have a few questions to ask you before I can offer you the position." She walked around the counter and disappeared through a door behind it. Flora hesitated, not knowing if she should leave her suitcase or take it with her.

Iris looked up. "Go on and get it over with. I'll mind your bag."

Flora left the suitcase and went to the door and knocked.

"Entrez," Chantal called.

"Good luck," Daisy called. "I hope you give her all the right answers."

Flora winked. "Of course I will. I'll just lie through my teeth."

"You'll do," Iris remarked drily. "You have the ethos of this place down to T already."

Chapter 3

The office was flooded with light. The half-open French window overlooked a small courtyard with tubs of roses and a small seating arrangement against an old stone wall.

Chantal was sitting behind a white desk crammed with photos and brochures. A laptop sat on a small table at the side. The white walls were bare except for two small Provençal landscapes in glowing jewel colours on the wall beside the desk.

"Gabriel Sardou," Chantal said and pointed at the paintings with her pencil. "Famous Provençal landscape artist."

"Lovely colours."

"Yes. Beautiful." Chantal waved at a chair in front of the desk. "Sit down."

Flora sat down on the edge of the chair and wrapped her legs around each other, trying to stop herself from shaking. No need to make it obvious how desperately she needed this job. She straightened her back and cleared her throat, ready to answer the questions.

"So…" Chantal slipped a pair of glasses onto her perfect nose and opened a folder. "Flora McKenna…thirty-two years old with eight years' experience in the field," she said in perfect but heavily accented English. She peered at Flora over the rim of her glasses. "Is that all correct?"

Flora nodded. "The agency I was working for closed down—that's why I lost my job. I was actually the manager there for the past two years."

"I know. I've done a little research. I also know you were good at your job in Dublin and managed to sell a lot of houses sold even during the recession."

Flora nodded. "Yes. Not my fault the agency went belly up."

"Possibly," Chantal mumbled and went back to her notes. "Not much more here except I gather your French is up to scratch. But, as we say in France, *la verité—*"

"*Est au fond de la marmite*," Flora filled in without thinking.

Chantal nodded, looking satisfied. "Excellent. But speaking good French isn't so important for your job. If you work here, you'll be dealing with anglophones. My clientele is mainly British, Irish and some Americans. A few Germans and Dutch people too, but Iris deals with them as she speaks fluent German."

"If," Flora muttered to herself.

"Just a few more questions," Chantal snapped. "I run a very good agency with quick sales, and we get the asking price too, mostly. So I can't hire anyone who sticks too closely to silly little moral principles."

Flora stared at Chantal. "What moral principles?"

"Oh, nothing serious. Just, well, we don't need to tell the truth, the whole truth and nothing but the truth all the time, if you get my meaning."

"Uh, yes."

"So," Chantal breezed on, "tell me…how would you go about showing a very small house?"

Flora thought for a moment. "For a start, I'd make sure the house had been cleared of clutter and recommend to the sellers they clean the house from top to bottom a week or so before the viewing. And also make sure the house smelled fresh and clean."

Chantal nodded.

"And then," Flora continued, feeling there was a lot more

to the question, "while showing the house, I'd make sure the prospective buyers arrived one by one so the house wouldn't be too crowded and look smaller than it is. And I'd make the buyers enter each room ahead of me, of course."

Chantal nodded. "Of course. But if there was a minor problem with the house and you knew about it, would you mention it?"

"Such as?"

"Oh…" Chantal waved her hand in the air, "you know, like a little damp here and there or a tile or two missing from the roof. Tiny flaws, really."

"Not small things like that. In any case, don't most people have their houses surveyed before they buy?"

"Not around here. How about noisy neighbours?"

"No. That would be silly. We operated very much with the 'buyers beware concept' in our agency. You have to highlight the positive and try to hide minor flaws."

"Quite right." Chantal paused.

"So," she continued, studying Flora while she spoke. "What about planning permission? I mean if the buyer should want to extend the house or add something and you needed permission to do so?"

"In Ireland, houses are often sold subject to planning."

Chantal looked confused. "Subject to…?"

"It means the house wouldn't be sold unless planning permission was granted," Flora explained. "Or the buyer would pay a deposit and that would be paid back if the permission was rejected."

Chantal gave a slight shiver of revulsion. "We wouldn't do that here. The question I wanted you to answer was…if the buyer expressed a wish to extend or rebuild, what would you tell them?"

There was a long pause. This was a tricky question. Flora knew at once that her answer would decide whether or not she got the job. It would decide the rest of her life, as melodramatic as it seemed. She thought for a moment, weighing up the pros and cons. If she said she would always tell buyers the truth about a house that couldn't be touched by builders if there was a problem, she would walk out of there dragging her suitcase back to the train station. Or be looking for a job as nanny or maid with a puny salary. But this was about telling lies to people who were buying a dream of living in the sun and who might get into big trouble with French planning laws and lose a lot of money. She pushed away the thought along with all her principles as she looked out at the sun-filled courtyard and the scent of roses filled the room.

"I'd tell them it would probably be allowed," she said, willing Chantal to believe her.

Chantal nodded. "What they don't know won't hurt them. Until a lot later, of course. But that doesn't happen very often."

"How often? "Flora couldn't help asking.

"Oh, now and then," Chantal said airily. She closed her folder. "Très bien. We've covered just about everything. You can tell Iris you've got the job, and she'll give you the contract and explain salary details and so on. I suggest you open an account with Societé Générale. They have an office around the corner." She rose and held out her hand. "Welcome to Agence du Soleil."

Flora took her hand. "Oh, thank you so much," she said and nearly burst into tears. The job was hers. She was now officially living in the south of France. Well, she would be as soon as she had somewhere to stay, but that was just a detail. How wonderful. How absolutely unbelievable.

"You can start in the morning. Just office work for now," Chantal said.

"Of course," Flora said and floated out of the office on a pink cloud of happiness.

* * *

Flora had only fleetingly thought about finding somewhere to live. Getting the job being the biggest obstacle, the problem of her accommodation was something she thought she would tackle once the interview was over. Dazed and happy, she walked out of Chantal's office to reclaim her suitcase and drag it to the nearest hotel. Once there, she would look for rooms to rent in the local newspaper and, hopefully, find something suitable. But Daisy solved the problem instantly.

"So, I see you got the job," she said when Flora came out.

Flora gave a start. "How did you know?"

Daisy laughed. "From the grin on your face. You look as if you've just won the lotto. So you passed the test then?"

"I suppose so."

Daisy took off her earphones. "Congratulations. And welcome to Happy Valley." She turned to Iris. "Hey, Iris, she got it."

Iris didn't take her eyes off the screen. "Of course she did. Just like us, darling. We're all ready to sell our souls to the devil to live in paradise." She turned to look at Flora. "Where are you staying?"

"I don't know yet," Flora replied. "I thought I'd go to a hotel and then look in the newspaper to see if I can find something to rent. Or even a room in a flat or whatever."

"You can bunk up with me," Daisy said. "I rent a flat in an old house just off Port de la Salis. That's between Antibes and the Cap, further out. The rent's horrendous, so sharing the cost with someone would be a great help. I should really try to find something cheaper. But it's such a great place I can't bear to leave. You'll have your own bedroom and then there's mine, a bathroom, a tiny room the landlord calls a kitchen, a living room and balcony overlooking the bay. The rent would be six hundred a month. What do you say?"

Flora hesitated. "Six hundred a month for a room?"

Daisy shrugged. "Yeah, I know, but this is Antibes and it's a good area."

Flora looked at Iris. "But I don't know what my salary will be yet, so—"

"You can't afford it," Iris said. "Unless you don't want to buy clothes or food or have any fun."

"I'll have a look at it in any case," Flora said, the euphoria of being employed slowly fizzling out.

"That might not be very wise," Iris warned. "Even on a bad day, Daisy's place is fabulous."

"And on a good day?" Flora couldn't help asking.

"Then it's heaven."

* * *

The late-Victorian villa stood, surrounded by modern monstrosities, like a tall lily in a field of weeds. After getting off the shuttle bus at the corner of the coast road and Avenue de la Mer, Flora quickly found the house and looked up at the white façade and the frieze with bunches of grapes and flowers around the top windows. It was one of the most beautiful houses she had ever seen. A small front garden with two palm trees and a bougainvillea spilling a riot of purple flowers over the wall led to wide steps up to a double door with stained-glass panels. All the windows had green louvred shutters that were closed against the evening sun. Could this be the right house? She consulted the piece of paper Daisy had given her and looked at the sign beside the gate that read *Villa Mon Rève:* the house of my dreams. What an apt name. And the right house, she realised, as she saw a window fly open on the top floor and Daisy hanging out, waving.

"There you are! I thought you'd got lost," Daisy shouted. "Come on up. I opened a bottle of wine and got a pizza."

The entrance hall was blissfully cool after the heat and humidity outside. Flora rolled her suitcase behind her across the marble floor and started to lug it up the stairs. She stopped as she heard voices coming from the half-open door of the ground-floor apartment. A dark head appeared and a young man in jeans and a denim jacket looked her up and down.

Daisy smiled. "*Bonjour,*" she said.

He nodded. "*Bonjour.* Are you Daisy's new flatmate?" he asked.

"I'm just going to look at the room for now. I'll decide when I see it," Flora said primly, finding herself slipping into French more easily than she had thought she could.

"I'm sure you'll be seduced," he replied with a wink.

"Do you live here?"

"No. I'm just visiting my grandparents. They own the building. I'm Bruno, by the way. And who are you?"

"Flora McKenna. From Dublin."

He smiled. "Nice name. I like Dublin. I've been there a few times. Great city. The music, the beer the—how do you say—craque?"

Flora laughed. "Yes. That's what we call it. You know Dublin well, I gather."

"Slightly. I'm sure there's more to it than what we tourists see."

"That's true." Flora gripped the handle of her suitcase and started up the stairs again. "I'd better get up there."

She could hear the door of the apartment on the top floor open and Daisy shouting something.

"What?" Flora shouted back. "I can't hear you."

Daisy clattered down the stairs. "I was just asking what was keeping you. But I see that Bruno's greeting you in his usual polite way."

Bruno smiled. "Hello, Daisy," he said in English. "When are you going to learn French?"

"When are you going to learn manners?" Daisy retorted. "How about helping Flora with her suitcase? Can't you see it's very heavy?"

"But she looks so strong," Bruno remarked. "I'm sure she can handle a little thing like a suitcase."

"Yeah, right, you wimp," Daisy muttered and grabbed the suitcase. "I suppose you're not up for it anyway. Come on, Flora. Don't just stand there looking at Bruno."

"Maybe she has better taste than you," Bruno suggested. He winked at Flora. "I like Irish girls. Especially blondes."

Flora blushed. "You speak very good English," was all she managed.

"It's not as good as your French. How come you speak it so well?"

"I spent a few summers in Paris, minding kids. I speak kids' French," Flora added with a laugh. "I know all the bad words. You'd be surprised how foul-mouthed the children of the wealthy can be."

Bruno laughed. "*Pas du tout.* Probably spoilt and never punished."

"That's for sure," Flora agreed.

"Hey, are you two going to stand out there all night and talk?" Daisy complained. "Come, on, for Pete's sake, Flora!"

Bruno sprang into action. "I'll take your suitcase." He grabbed it and sprinted up the stairs ahead of them and into the apartment, reappearing seconds later. "*Voilá*, your *valise* is in the spare room. I have to go or my *mamie* will be very angry. She'll have dinner ready very soon." He kissed his fingers at Flora. "*A bientôt, ma belle.* See you later, Daisy," he added and bounded down the stairs.

"Now, that's something I've never seen before," Daisy remarked. "Bruno being *polite*."

"You don't seem to like him much."

Daisy smirked. "Like him? Nah, I loathe him. He's very good in bed, though. Hottest boyfriend I've ever had."

Flora stared at Daisy. "He's your boyfriend?"

Daisy closed the front door of the apartment. "Yes. Weird, but that's Frenchmen for you. Love, hate, hot, cold, shouts and kisses. Very intense and dramatic. Tiring but never boring."

"Really? I don't know if I could cope with that."

Daisy laughed. "Find yourself a Frenchman and find out. But, hey, come in and see the flat. Then tell me if you'd like to stay."

Without moving from the hall, Flora glanced into the big living room at the end of which she could see spectacular views of the sapphire-blue sea of the bay and the mountains beyond through a large picture window. She looked back at Daisy and laughed. "You devil. You knew I wouldn't be able to resist. Of course I'll stay."

* * *

Much later, over pizza and wine on the terrace, Flora felt as if she had known Daisy for a long time and that the flat had been waiting for her all her life. She drained her glass and munched the last bit of crust of her pizza and sighed as she looked out over the bay in the gathering dusk. The lights around the shore were beginning to glow, and the bay was soon edged by pinpricks of lights, like a pearl necklace on the edge of a blue velvet dress. "What a wonderful view. I don't think I'll ever get tired of it. I feel as if I was meant to be here, somehow."

Daisy poured the last drops of wine into Flora's glass. "I know. That's how I felt when I came here. Of course, I could never afford to live here alone, so I have to share. But I've always been lucky with my roommates."

"I'll try to live up to that," Flora promised. "I'm quite tidy. Not to the point of being perfect, but I try not to be too much of a slob. My room's so pretty, I'd hate to spoil the look of it."

"It was done by Bruno's grandmother. She's a painter and a textile designer. The curtains and bedspreads are her work. And the rugs."

"I love the pastel colours. They really go with the sea and the views of the hills behind the house."

"Very nice," Daisy agreed. "But tell me about yourself, Flora. The story of your life and all that crap."

"You first. I'm dying to know what brought you here."

Daisy shrugged and ran her finger along the edge of her glass. "What brought me here? You want to know how a girl from Brooklyn ended up in a real estate agency in Antibes? What takes women anywhere? A man, of course. Not Bruno. I met him only six months ago. No, it was a guy I met at a party in Manhattan. I'd just broken up with someone and was kind of vulnerable, I guess. On the rebound, wanting to prove to myself I still had it, whatever 'it' is. I was in a dead-end job, working as personal assistant to a bitch in a corporate office. I was ripe for a life makeover, you might say. I'd just turned thirty, as well. You know, when you're beginning to realise you'll never reach that goal you set out for yourself when you leave college." Daisy shot a glance at Flora. "But maybe you're not there yet?"

"Of course I am," Flora replied. "I'm thirty-two and was unemployed until this morning. And relationships? Yeah, been there too. The great career and two point four children didn't materialise. And there was this man—" She stopped. "I don't want to go into it right now. But I know where you're coming from."

"I'm sure there are more women like us than we know." Daisy turned to look up at the stars that were beginning to glimmer in the dark sky. "It's out there, though, isn't it? Our destiny. That one thing we need to be complete. If only we could find it." She shook herself and looked back at Flora. "But to get back to moi…"

"Yes?" Flora leaned back in her chair and sipped her wine, waiting for Daisy's' story. She was so pretty, with her light-blonde hair and sparkly blue eyes—so alluring and fun. She must have had an interesting past.

"You'll laugh when I tell you this," Daisy said. "But my hottest love affair was a virtual one."

Flora sat up. "What? On the Internet?"

Daisy nodded. "Yes. God, this sounds so pathetic. But like a lot of people, I found myself so alone in a big city. I worked hard all day and then didn't have the strength to go out to a club or pub to meet people. So I sat in bed, with my laptop and chatted on the Internet. Facebook, of course. I joined one of those groups. I think it was for fans of detective stories."

"Yes? Go on. You connected with a man who reads detective stories?"

Daisy sighed. "No. I wish. It was an author. He'd written this series of hard-boiled thrillers. God, what a jerk. Except I didn't realise it at the time. He was so sweet and kind of corny, you know? Posted a picture of Humphrey Bogart as his profile. So, then I kind of believed he really was some kind of reincarnation of Bogie and that I was chatting to *him*. And the chats got hotter and hotter. Sometimes, I felt as if we were dating and that we were actually having sex. He said such sweet things to me. Told me how much he wanted to meet me, how much he wanted to sleep with me. Only problem was, he lived in California."

"So you never met?"

"No. And we knew we never would. He said he thought we'd meet in another, spiritual life. That we were kindred spirits and that our relationship was meant to happen in another world."

"Sounds kind of dreamy."

Daisy sighed. "It was. In fact, I thought not meeting was a good thing. Fantasies are often better than reality. It lasted two years, believe it or not. I didn't want it to end. We were getting to know each other in a way I've never known anyone before. Because we never met in real life, we dared to reveal the most intimate things about ourselves…" Her voice trailed away and her face, in the dim light of the full moon, was sad.

"But it ended?" Flora said, not wanting to intrude but still needing to know.

"Yes. We had an argument. I didn't agree with his political views. And then I discovered he was both a homophobe and sexist. His attitude to women was appalling. I didn't realise it at first, but then I noticed how he saw women as sexual objects. Old-fashioned, of course. But not surprising once I discovered he was a lot older than he first told me. I thought he was in his forties, but it turned out he was in his sixties."

"Oh, wow. That must have been a bit of a shock."

Daisy shrugged. "Yes, in a way. But I wouldn't have minded had he told me in the first place. I'm not ageist. It was the fact that he lied to me that was the worst thing. Anyway, that made me realise online friendships aren't a good idea. And that real life is so much better than sitting at home posting on Facebook. So, I started going out more. And then I was invited to a party in Manhattan."

"And met a Frenchman?" Flora asked.

Daisy giggled. "No. He was Greek. Gorgeous hunk, you know, like one of those guys in a commercial for men's cologne. Total cliché, really. But we had fun—nothing serious, actually. I was still sad and confused after my Internet experience, but Giorgos was just what the doctor ordered. He was in New York on vacation, and when it was time for him to leave, I decided to go with him. He was working in a Greek restaurant in Nice. So I came here and then, when that romance ended, decided to stay. I got a job with Chantal and the rest, as they say, is history." Daisy stretched her arms over her head. "So here I am, living it up on the Riviera, working my butt off in a dead-end job that pays peanuts and in a relationship with a domineering bastard. Couldn't be happier, really"

Flora couldn't help laughing.

Daisy lowered her arms and peered at Flora in the dim light. "But, hey, what about you? What's your story?"

"Me? Not much of a story."

"Ah, come on, I can tell there's some saucy stuff in your past. You have that naughty look."

Flora laughed. "That's what I was always told at school. Must be the gap between my front teeth. Makes me look cheeky."

"It's cute. But go on," Daisy urged. "Spill."

Flora hesitated. There was so much in her past she wanted to forget. So much she wished she hadn't done.

"I never think before I leap," she said. "I think with my heart, lead with my chin and never worry about the consequences. This has landed me in some very tricky situations and made me fall in love with a man who—" Flora stopped, unable to go on. They had only just met, and unlike Daisy, she couldn't share details of her love life with a stranger. In any case, it was too soon and too painful to talk about. She stifled a yawn. "Can I tell you tomorrow? I'm exhausted, and I haven't even unpacked my bag yet."

Daisy sprang to her feet. "God, I'm so insensitive. Here you are, listening to the dumb story of my life after what must have been a very long day. Go and unpack and then have a bath. I'll clean up here."

Flora got up and took her plate and glass. "I'll take this into the kitchen on my way."

"Thanks, but don't worry about the rest. I'll just stick it all into the dishwasher."

Flora put her plate on the kitchen counter and continued into her room, where her suitcase had been put on a bench by the window. She paused for a moment, looking at the moonlight pouring in through the window, illuminating the big bed, the white chest of drawers and the light-blue rug on the wooden floor. Then she switched on the light by the bed, and the room was at once bathed in a soft light. She went to the window and closed the shutters and then turned her attention to her suitcase. She would just fish out her toiletries and nightgown and unpack the rest in the morning. Looking forward to getting into the bed that Daisy had so kindly made with clean sheets, Flora zipped open the lid of the suitcase. She did a double take as she looked at the contents, just as Daisy bounced into the room with a pile of fluffy white towels in her arms.

"What's the matter? Is something missing?"

Flora turned to look at Daisy. "I've no idea."

"What do you mean?"

"This isn't my suitcase."

Chapter 4

Daisy dropped the towels on the bed and looked into the suitcase. "Oh, gee, no. Not what I'd expect to see you unpack. Except if you were the butch type who wears men's underwear. Fancy stuff, though. Calvin Klein, no less. And Cardin shirts."

"But what about my stuff?" Flora wailed. "My clothes and shoes and things"

"How come you didn't open the suitcase until now? Didn't you stay in a hotel in Nice the first night?"

"I had my night things in the carry-on bag. Couldn't be bothered to unpack until now. But I need my stuff. What am I going to do?"

"Find out who owns this one," Daisy suggested. "Maybe contact the airport? Whoever took yours might have returned it."

Flora searched in her handbag for her phone. "Yes. That's what I should do. I'll find the number on Google."

"Didn't you put anything on your suitcase to identify it?" Daisy asked. "I mean a black canvas Samsonite...must be the most common of all."

"I did, of course. A light-blue ribbon tied to the handle, just like this one. Feck! This guy must have done the same." She Googled 'Nice Airport, luggage'.

"Philippe Belcourt," Daisy said. "Nice name."

Flora looked up from her phone. "What? Who's that?"

Daisy showed Flora a book she had taken out of the case. "The owner of this suitcase, I suppose. Gee, the fancy type who writes his name into his books."

"What did you say the name was again?"

"Philippe Belcourt."

"I know that name from somewhere." Flora racked her brain as a faint memory floated around in her mind. Then she remembered. "I know who he is! The man I spoke to on the plane just before we disembarked. We chatted for a bit while we waited for the doors to open. He gave me his card."

"Do you still have it?"

"God, I don't know." Flora searched her shirt pocket. "Not here." She dug into her handbag. Nothing.

"What about that little pocket of your cute linen jacket?"

"Don't think so." Flora lifted the jacket she had flung on the bed and stuck her hand into the pocket. Her fingers found a crumpled piece of paper. She pulled it out, grinning at Daisy. "Here it is—his card."

Daisy snatched it away and peered at it. "*Philippe Belcourt. Photographe.* Address in Vence. And a phone number. Let's call him."

Flora looked at her watch. "But it's nearly midnight. A bit too late to call?"

"Not in France. Is he young and good-looking?"

"Not young. Late forties, I'd guess. Good-looking? Yes… in a battered, lived-in sort of way."

"He sounds sexy. I'm sure he'll be still up. Maybe on a hot date with some gorgeous older woman."

"In that case, maybe we shouldn't disturb him?"

"On the contrary." Daisy chuckled and pulled her phone out of the pocket of her shorts. Before Flora could stop her, Daisy had dialled the number. Someone replied instantly.

"Hello," Daisy said. "Is this Philippe Belcourt? I'm very sorry to disturb you, but I'm calling about your suitcase… no, I don't have it, but my friend…just a moment, I'll put her on." Daisy handed the phone to Flora. "He's annoyed," she mouthed. "Tell him how upset you are."

Flora backed away from the phone. "Hang up," she whispered. "We'll call him in the morning."

"No. Talk to him. He wants his suitcase. He might have yours."

"Oh, okay." Swallowing hard, Flora took the phone. "Hello," she croaked. "This is Flora McKenna. We met on the plane and—"

"Yes, yes, I remember," Philippe Belcourt growled. "But it's very late. How come you've only just discovered you have my suitcase?"

"I…well, I didn't get a chance to unpack until very late."

"I see." He paused. "I suppose the one I have here is yours, then? It seems to belong to a woman, in any case."

"What does it look like?" Flora asked without thinking.

"Exactly like mine. It even has a nearly identical blue ribbon tied to the handle. Why isn't there a name on it?"

Flora frowned. "It should have. I put a label on it at the check-out desk."

"Must have been ripped off. I'm afraid I opened it. Thought it was mine, but then I saw all the female frou-frou in there, so I realised I must have picked up the wrong one."

"So," Flora started. "What's in it?"

"I haven't really looked at it in detail. But I have it here, right in front of me."

"Could you open it and have look and tell me?" Flora asked.

"D'accord. Just a moment. Uh, underwear at the top. Two white bras, size…" He paused. "36B. A white T-shirt with the logo 'I'm too sexy for my shirt', a—"

Flora blushed. "It's mine. No need to look at anything else."

"Not even a copy of Fifty Shades of Grey?" he teased.

"Uh, oh, yeah…well, I bought that for research. Wanted to see what all the fuss was about. I haven't read it yet."

"I'm sure it's very good." He cleared his throat. "But, ma chère Mademoiselle McKenna, we have to figure out how to exchange our suitcases."

"Yes."

"Tonight's too late, I'm afraid. But tomorrow?"

"Yes?" Flora kicked herself. Why was she standing there saying nothing but 'yes'? "Can you come here? To Antibes? I'm in a flat in a house on Avenue de la Mer."

"Avenue de la Mer? Oh. Sorry, I can't explain now, but it's not convenient for me. I can meet you further up the coast road. If you take the bus," he continued, "and get off at the *rond point*."

"I know where it is."

"There's a café there, called Café Rosmarin. We could meet there at…eleven o'clock?"

"That would be fine," Flora said.

"Très bien," he said. "See you then, Mademoiselle."

"What did he say?" Daisy asked when Flora hung up.

"We're meeting at this café up the road to do the exchange tomorrow." Her face fell. "But I'm supposed to start at the agency then. What am I going to do?"

"I'll cover for you until you have it all sorted. That okay?"

"Uh, yes. Thanks." Flora frowned, her mind still on the phone call. "I told him where I was but he said he couldn't come here. 'Not convenient' he said."

"How gentlemanly of him."

"I have a feeling he's a lot of things," Flora mused. "But a gentleman is not one of them."

* * *

Flora got off the bus with the suitcase and squinted in the bright sunshine. It was already so hot she felt sweat break out on her upper lip. But the café was right in front of her, so she trundled the suitcase inside, where the air conditioning had cooled the temperature by at least ten degrees. Except for a girl behind the counter, the café was deserted. Flora looked at her watch. He was late. She ordered an espresso and sat down at a table by the window, looking at the people passing by outside. People-watching in France, especially on the Riviera, was always fun. This part of Antibes was full of shops and restaurant, and on a Saturday, most people were out and about, shopping, meeting friends for coffee or buying the compulsory baguette for lunch. Sometimes they did all three, Flora noticed, as she watched a very chic woman with a stick of bread under her arm and two bags with boutique logos kiss another woman on both cheeks before they both settled at a table under the awning outside. Dressed in white shorts and silk tops, they didn't seem to notice the heat. Flora wondered if she would ever be like them: effortlessly elegant and confident. Not very likely. She would never rid herself of the feeling her shape was unfashionable. And she would never have hair like that: sleek, superbly cut and artfully ruffled.

"*Bonjour,*" a voice said in her ear.

Flora jumped and looked up. There he was, standing beside her table, dressed in jeans and a blue shirt, his sunglasses on top of his head, looking at her with his warm brown eyes.

"Good morning," she said and held out her hand.

"Good morning." He ignored her hand and sat down, clicked his fingers at the waitress and ordered an espresso. "Your suitcase is in my car parked down the street. We'll make the exchange as soon as I've had my coffee."

"Okay," Flora said. It was strange to sit like this with him, seeing him up close, meeting his eyes and trying to find something intelligent to say. "Lovely day."

"As usual." His sudden smile lit up his face and made his eyes, surrounded by a myriad of laughter lines, twinkle mischievously. "Strange to meet again, isn't it?"

"Yes."

"Maybe it was meant to happen?"

Flora shrugged. "Who knows?" She knew she was coming across as surly and boring, but she had no idea how to behave with someone like him: suave, elegant and a lot older than her. He wasn't old enough to be a father figure or young enough to fall in love with, but she nevertheless felt a surge of attraction when their eyes met. What was going on? Did he feel attracted to her, too? Or was he just playing games? Maybe it was a thing with Frenchmen, this flirty look and cheeky smile, making any woman feel pretty and desirable. Unable to bear the tension any more, she stood up so suddenly, she knocked into the table and made his coffee splash onto his shirt.

"*Merde!*" He jumped up and started to dab the wet stain with a napkin. "Why did you do that?"

"No reason," Flora said, emboldened by his anger. "I just thought that shirt would look good with a little coffee splashed on it."

He laughed. "You're an unusual girl, Flora. Most women would have said 'Oh, I'm so sorry, it was an accident' or something like that. But you make it into a joke."

Flora shrugged. "Yeah, why not? I obviously didn't do it on purpose, so why pretend to be sorry? I'm not the doormat type. Maybe that's why I haven't had much luck in love?"

He stopped dabbing. "You haven't? With your pretty, freckly face, lovely green eyes and those legs?"

Flora tugged at her skirt. "Men want women to be submissive. They pretend they don't, but it always comes out sooner or later. Mostly later. Too much later, when you're committed and start dreaming about a life together." She stopped. "Don't know why I said that. Forget it. Let's go and get my suitcase and get this over with. I'm sure you're dying to get as far away from me as possible." She drew breath.

"Not at all. But I have to get going, anyway." He threw the

napkin and a ten-euro bill on the table. "That will cover both our coffees." He took the suitcase and dragged it out of the café and up the street towards a small parking lot, Flora in his wake. They came to a stop in front of a red, convertible, Mercedes sports car with cream leather seats. Flora stared at it. Was this his car? It had to be. Her suitcase was crammed into the small space behind the seats.

He took out an electronic key from his pocket. "*Voilà*. My car." He was about to lift his suitcase when he was interrupted by his phone. He pulled it out of the pocket of his jeans. "Excuse me," he said and put it to his ear. "Oui?" He listened intently for a while, then, "J'arrive, toute de suite." He hung up and turned to Flora. "I have to go. Urgent business. I'll drive you as close to your house as I can, as I'm going past on my way out to the Cap. I can drop you off at the beach at Port de la Salis, and then you only have a short walk—"

"Pity you couldn't have done that in the first place," Flora couldn't help remarking. "Would have saved me a lot of effort."

He shrugged. "Yes, yes, I know. I wasn't being rude. I'm on a very tight schedule today, and if I go up that street—"

"Your car will burst into flames?"

He smiled thinly. "No. I'll have to drive around in that maze of one-way streets before getting back to the main road, that's all. So dropping you off at the beach will save me a lot of time. I hope that's not awkward for you."

Flora shrugged. "No big deal. It's just a short walk from there." She opened the passenger door and slid into the seat, sighing with pleasure as she felt the smooth leather against her legs. "Oooh, sexy," she purred. "I've always wanted to sit in one of these."

"Lucky I parked in the shade," he remarked and got into the driver's seat. "Otherwise the hot leather would have burned that milky white skin."

"I know." Flora glanced at her legs. "They're so white. I should apply some fake tan. I really stick out here in the land of gloss and glamour."

He eyed her legs. "Your skin is beautiful. Like alabaster. Don't change it."

"Uh, thanks." Flora sidled away. "So, does this car actually move?"

"Of course." He inserted the key and the engine started with a low purring sound. He backed out of the parking lot, and they were soon cruising down Boulevard James Wyllie, which ran along the shore and around Point Bacon out toward Cap d'Antibes.

From her bucket seat, Flora gazed out at the golden sand of the beaches, the blue-green sea of the bay and the snow-capped Alps in the distance. Philippe turned on the car radio, and a French song wafted out of the loudspeaker. With the wind in her hair, the song in her ears combined with the beautiful vistas, Flora experienced a moment of absolute bliss. She turned her head and looked at Philippe— his handsome profile, strong hands on the wheel and muscular forearms—and wished this moment wouldn't end. But it did. Too soon for Flora, they arrived at the Port de la Salis, where sailing boats were moored in the marina and a small crowd had gathered at the ice-cream kiosk.

Philippe pulled up at the kerb. With the engine idling, he got out, opened Flora's door and lifted out her suitcase. They stood there, looking at each other for a moment.

"I forgot to ask," he said. "Did you get the job?"

"Yes. I'm working at an estate agency. *Agence du Soleil*."

"I know the one you mean. I took a few pictures for them a while ago." Philippe glanced at his watch. "I have to go. Goodbye, Flora." Before she had a chance to react, he kissed her on both cheeks.

"Uh, goodbye," she said. "Nice to meet you again."

"Very nice." He slid in behind the wheel, slammed the door and drove off.

Flora stood there in the hot sunshine, staring at the Mercedes disappearing up the hill, wondering if she had just woken up from a dream.

* * *

"He must be loaded," Daisy said when Flora told her about her morning.

"Maybe he borrowed the car?" Flora suggested.

"Who lends a car like that to anyone?"

"I suppose nobody would." Flora carried her suitcase to her room. "I have to unpack. Then you can have your pyjamas back and I can change my clothes. What a relief I found my suitcase and it's not on its way to Istanbul or something."

"I wonder what kind of photography he does?" Daisy said. "I mean, how does he earn the kind of money to buy a car like that?"

"No idea. He said he took pictures for our agency a while back."

"That wouldn't earn him megabucks. I'm sure he's into something a lot more lucrative."

"Probably. But I suppose we'll never find out."

Daisy picked up her phone. "I'm going to Google him."

"Okay. Let me know if you find anything." Flora went into her room to unpack her suitcase and change her clothes. Twenty minutes later, as she put the last items into the chest of drawers, she heard Daisy call.

"What's up?" Flora asked when she returned to the living room.

"I found him." Daisy chortled and held up her smartphone to Flora. "Look, he's here, on Google. He seems to be a very well-known nature and landscape photographer. He's published some of those expensive coffee-table books with gorgeous photos. Iceland, Alaska, Bali…he seems to have been everywhere. But does that earn you mega bucks?"

"I wonder what he was doing in Ireland," Flora mused. "Maybe he's going to do a book about Irish landscapes?"

"Nah. Must have been up to something fishy over there."

"He doesn't look fishy."

"Of course not." Daisy winked. "He looks completely innocent. They're the worst."

* * *

Flora had little chance to find out anything else about Philippe Belcourt during the following week. After a leisurely Sunday spent walking in the hills, followed by a few hours on the beach, she was ready to face her first day at the agency. Dressed in white linen trousers and a green sleeveless top, Flora walked to the bus stop, enjoying the early morning freshness, the warm sunshine and the smell from the umbrella pines on the hill above the houses. That smell was something she knew she would always associate with Provence. She could see the marina, where the sailing boats swayed gently on the still water, hear the seagulls and the cicadas that were just beginning to chirp. She looked out across the bay and the blue waters at a lone sailboat in the distance. She wished she could be on it, sailing out to sea and the islands, instead of having to face her first day of work. But when the bus arrived, she got on board, looking forward to the challenges ahead. After a ten-minute ride, she got off at the stop just outside Agence du Soleil, where Iris was opening the shutters and unlocking the door.

She turned around as Flora approached. "Good morning. Where's Daisy?"

"She overslept. She'll be here in about twenty minutes or so."

Iris rolled her eyes. "As usual. Why can't she get her act together? She has an appointment to show a house at nine thirty. One of our most important clients. This house will fetch over a million, and if we miss that deal, Chantal will be apoplectic. Shit, and I have a doctor's appointment I can't miss. You'll have to go."

Daisy stiffened. "What? Me? But I can't. I don't know where to go or what to do. I mean, I don't know the ropes yet. I haven't a clue how the French property market works, what with the notaire and the contracts and stuff. Chantal said I was to read up on that during my first week."

"Chantal won't be here until later. When Daisy comes, I'll have to go to the doctor's and then she'll have to mind the office until we both come back. Look, it's not about signing contracts, it's about showing a house. Surely you can manage that?"

Flora suddenly noticed how pale Iris was. Maybe she was ill. If it was just about showing a house, it wouldn't be a problem. She had showed thousands of houses during her time at the Dublin agency, and she was good at it.

"Okay," she said. "I'll go. Just tell me where it is and give me the keys, a map and the brochures."

"Great." Iris walked into the office and searched among the papers and brochures on her desk. "It's on the Cap. Beautiful house near La Garoupe. You can take the shuttle there from the terminus off the square. The client's name is…" She flicked through her diary. "Ross Fitzgerald. He's American, I think. Don't know much about him. Chantal took the call when he contacted us. Probably some old geezer who wants to spend his twilight years in a sunny place. I'm sure you can charm him."

"I'll do my best." Flora took the stack of papers.

"The house is a little bit run-down and needs updating. But do your best to point out the advantages. And if you get there before the buyer, you can open shutters and push the furniture around a bit to make it look good. I'm sure you know what I mean."

Flora nodded. "Yes, we used to call that covering up the cracks in our agency. You can even sidle into a room, stand in front of a damp spot on the wall and point out the view of the garden or something."

"Exactly. And have a sniff around and make sure there's no smell of damp or drains. I think there's an air freshener in the kitchen that we used the last time we showed it. You'd better get going. You need out be out there in about forty-five minutes. You can read up on the house on your way."

"Okay." Flora stuffed the keys and papers into her bag. "I'll see you later."

"Take a coffee break when you've finished. There's a little café by the beach. It's beautiful out there."

"I will. Thanks."

Flora caught the little shuttle bus just as it left the terminus. She read through the brochure on the way out to the Cap d'Antibes and looked at the photos. Lovely house with spectacular views situated right at the tip of the cap, near the house of Jules Verne. From there, one could see both Juan les Pins to the west and the Bay of Angels and Nice to the east. The house itself, although not very big, was beautiful with big rooms and what looked like a large but overgrown garden. A dream house, despite its dilapidated state. Some elderly man would buy it and live there until the end of his days. Flora sighed wistfully. Some people had all the luck.

The bus drew up at the final stop. "The end of the line, Mademoiselle," the bus driver called, waking Flora from her daydream.

She smiled and nodded at him and jumped off the bus. The house was only a short walk from there, according to the map Iris had given her.

She walked into the hills, past the beautiful villas, with gardens full of fragrant flowers, majestic umbrella pines and gnarled olive trees. The older houses were the most beautiful, some of them over a hundred years old or more, pink, orange or a mellow cream, bougainvillea spilling over the walls in a riot of purple.

She came to a stop in front of a very old, abandoned house, white with green shutters, inside a high wall. This was the house she was looking for. The name of the house was *Les Temps Heureux*—The Happy Times—and it had a beautiful old garden with a swimming pool sitting in the dappled sunlight beside the terrace. The views of the headland and the bay were breathtaking. She had a feeling that the 'happy times' had been many and wonderful all through the years and that the house was waiting for another family to move in and start up those happy times all over again.

After the long walk, Flora regretted her choice of footwear. The sandals that would have been so cool in the office were chafing her heels. Deciding she would be more comfortable barefoot, she took them off before she opened the gate.

"These shoes weren't made for walking?" a voice said behind her.

Flora turned and saw a tall man coming up the hill. Looking lean and fit, he was dressed in a white T-shirt, blue shorts and scuffed boat shoes. His blond hair was ruffled by the wind, and when he took off his sunglasses, she noticed his eyes were as blue as the sea she could glimpse between the pine trees. He looked about her age.

"No. I think they were meant for sitting," she said, returning his broad grin.

He unscrewed the cap of the water bottle he was carrying and drank from it. "Hot day."

"Yes. I'm trying to get used to the heat here."

He held out the bottle. "Do you want a drink of water?"

"No, thanks. I have bottle of Evian in my bag."

"Of course you do. Silly of me."

"You're American?"

"No. Canadian."

"Sorry."

"No problem. We're used it." He turned and looked at the house. "Nice place."

"Lovely," Flora agreed. "It's for sale. I'm from the agency and I'm here to show it to a client. And old man who wants to end his years here in this beautiful place."

"A good place to do it," the man said.

"Yes." Flora took out a bunch of keys. "But if you'll excuse me, I have to go inside. The client will be here soon. I have about twenty minutes to go through the house and open the shutters. And I have to make it look a little more…" She stopped. Why was she telling this stranger her business? "Well whatever," she ended lamely.

"A little more attractive?" he enquired with a knowing look. "Hide the damp spots and the cracks and dents?"

Flora laughed. "Yes, I suppose."

"I don't see the point. This house doesn't need it."

"Probably not," Flora agreed. "But still…"

He beamed his wide grin at her again. "Enough fooling around." He held out his hand. "I'm your client."

Flora's jaw dropped. "What? You mean, you're—"

"Yes." He sighed theatrically. "I'm Ross Fitzgerald. The old man who's going to end his days here."

Chapter 5

Flora put her hand on her mouth to stifle a nervous giggle. "Shit, you're joking."

"Nope. I am he. Forgot to bring the wheelchair and the walking stick."

"You look young for your age," Flora said, in an attempt to cover her embarrassment with a lame joke.

"I know. Must be good genes or something. I'm really eighty-five, you know, even though I look a lot younger."

Flora laughed. "Amazing. Why did Iris think you'd be old?"

"No idea. But why are we standing here talking nonsense? Let's go in and see the house. Never mind the cracks and the damp. I'm more interested in the location. I might even decide to tear the house down and build a new one."

Flora dug around in her bag for the keys. "You're an architect? Or a builder?"

"No, not exactly. Although I am interested in architecture as an art form."

Flora found the keys and put one of them into the lock of the gate. It was rusty and the lock was stiff, but after a little fiddling around, the key finally turned and she pushed the gate open. "Here we are. Please go in."

Ross stood back. "After you, Mademoiselle."

The gate creaked as Flora pushed it open. "Thank you. Follow me."

They fell silent as they entered the garden. There was an instant feeling of peace and tranquillity as they walked into the cool shade of the umbrella pines. Flora closed the gates behind them and walked on the path covered in pine needles toward the front steps of the house.

"Bauhaus," Ross said, looking up at the plain white façade. "Or something very like it."

Flora consulted the brochure. "The house was built in nineteen twenty-eight."

"Aha. Well, that would fit with the period."

Flora followed his gaze. The house was built with clean lines and looked like a white cube with big windows cut in with geometrical precision. Devoid of any kind of ornamentation or embellishment, apart from the green shutters, it looked stark and cold to Flora at first. But when they went around the back and she saw how the house seemed to float above the lawn, light and airy, she appreciated its beauty and how it fitted in perfectly with the infinity of the blue skies and darker sapphire of the seas below. As she kept looking at the house, it seemed more classical than modern, with lines not unlike those of a Greek temple. Even though it was in need of repair, it still had a kind of dignity and ageless beauty.

"Stunning," Ross mumbled and took out his smartphone. "I'm going to take a few pictures before we go inside. I think this house needs a terrace at the back instead of that narrow ledge."

"Okay." Flora jangled the keys. "I'll go in and open the shutters." She went around to the front of the house, unlocked the green door and stepped inside. The white tiles of the hall floor were cool under her bare feet and in the half-light, she could see the shapes of a few bits of furniture that hadn't been removed by the previous owner. She touched a white table under a cracked mirror and jumped as a tiny lizard scuttled over her foot. She had the eerie feeling someone was watching her. She looked around and met the eyes of a child in a portrait hanging on the opposite wall. Flora moved closer and saw it was an old print of a Greek mosaic depicting a girl with a wreath of flowers in her hair that fell in ringlets to her shoulders. The hooded eyes gazing at Flora were full of mystery as if she was trying to convey a story across the span of thousands of years that had passed since the mosaic was made.

"Delos," Ross said.

Flora jumped. "You scared me!"

"Sorry. He gestured at the picture. "That's a copy of a mosaic in Delos in the Greek islands. I've seen it there, too. Come on, let's open the shutters and do a tour."

"Okay." Flora was about to start up the wide staircase when her phone rang. "Excuse me while I get this," she said.

Ross nodded and pointed up the stairs. "I'll go ahead," he mouthed.

Flora nodded and put the phone to her ear. "Hello?"

"Flora?" said Chantal's shrill voice. "Are you at the house?"

"Yes."

"With the client?"

"Yes."

"It's Monsieur Fitzgerald?"

"That's right."

"Mon Dieu, he's there already. Flora, he is a *very* important client. But the sellers have just called me and they've increased the price to two million."

"What? That seems like extortion to me."

"No, no, it's not. It's about the location and the building being an architectural gem. Don't worry, that man is very rich."

"But the house needs a lot of work," Flora argued. "And he wants to build a terrace and maybe an extension too."

Chantal laughed softly. "That might present a little

problem for him. I'm not sure he'll be allowed to add anything to the house. It's…how do you say…protected?"

"Listed?"

"That's right. Listed. But no matter. For the moment, show him the house and agree with everything, and tell him it will all be sorted out with the mayor."

"Will it?"

Chantal laughed ironically. "Probably not, except if I agree to sleep with him."

"Shit," Flora hissed into the phone. "What am I going to do? I don't feel like telling a lot of lies."

"Just be vague. I'm sure you can handle that. If you do a good job, I'll let you have a good share of the commission."

"I'll do my best."

"Très bien. Don't worry about it for now. Just one thing to remember—don't let him go upstairs."

* * *

Chantal hung up with a feeling of doom. That new girl was too honest and far too caring. She didn't seem to have the detachment needed for the job. The other girls—Daisy with her complicated love life and Iris with her personal problems—didn't care if they had to tell a lie or two. They breezed through a sale without much thought about the buyer's problems or worrying about ethics. It was a job, not a vocation. Kindness didn't come into it. Or worrying whether people could afford a house they wanted to buy. You would have thought working in the tough, Dublin, housing market might have hardened her. She would learn, though. But she shouldn't have been sent out to show that house so soon after arriving. It was a tricky sale with a lot of complications. They had hooked that buyer, whom she knew would buy if he thought he could make alterations to the house. She hoped Flora wouldn't reveal how difficult that would be. But that wasn't the biggest problem right now. The house shouldn't have been shown that day, before she could go and tidy up. Iris had made a mistake, but of course she was too preoccupied with her own problems to pay attention. Daisy had to go and oversleep, and there was nobody in charge. Now, Flora was showing the house before it was ready. They would go upstairs and then they would discover the room.

But would they know what was going on there? Or connect it with her? Probably not. She sighed and rolled her stiff shoulders. It was all the stress, of course. Nobody could live this way and not be stressed: a husband who was slowly sliding into a decline; running an agency where every sale was a struggle; and then this…this double life, her secret love affair. But that part of her life was her lifeline. It was what kept her from sinking into a black hole of despair.

She got up from her desk and stretched her back. So tired all the time. But what could she do? Put her husband into a home? No, it was unthinkable. She had been up twice during the night when he woke up confused, not knowing where he was. He was quite lucid during the day, and the new medication seemed to be improving his mood, but at night it was as if some kind of demon invaded his mind. It was so sad. Jean, a man not yet in his sixties, who should have been enjoying his golden years, losing his grip on reality. Caring for him was a heavy burden. But at least his temper tantrums were a thing of the past

They would be married thirty years in August. Chantal stared into to the courtyard, where the sunlight glittered on the carafe of water on the little table in the shade of the acacia tree. Thirty years. She had been twenty, studying business and marketing at the university in Nice, a young girl, looking into the future with confidence and hope. Jean, handsome and sweet, who became the love of her life. The memory of how they met was still vivid in her mind.

* * *

It was the third time Chantal was asked to be bridesmaid. Being superstitious, her mother warned her it might mean she would never be a bride.

"I don't believe in that nonsense," Chantal scoffed as she put on her bridesmaid's dress, a dream in blue silk that skimmed her body and made her eyes sparkle. "And wouldn't anyone risk it to wear this dress? It's Dior, after all, and when will I ever get the chance to wear such a dress again?"

"Don't say I didn't warn you," her mother replied with doom in her voice.

Chantal laughed, pinned a few white roses into her dark curls, kissed her mother and floated to the car that was to take her to pick up the bride and the other bridesmaids. She was twenty years old and on the threshold of her adult life. She didn't care about marriage and a steady boyfriend. She enjoyed her freedom, her friends and the business course at the college in Nice.

The wedding mass took place in the old church in St Tropez and the reception at the bride's home in Ramautelle, where the buffet was laid out on a terrace overlooking the deep-blue waters of the bay of Pampelonne. The bride's family was from St Tropez aristocracy, who had lived and grown wine in the region for generations.

Chantal mingled with childhood friends and new acquaintances from university. She knew nearly everyone at the party, and when she spotted an unfamiliar man in the crowd around the buffet, she was immediately intrigued. The fact that he was tall and very handsome had a lot to do with her interest, but it was his kind eyes and lovely smile that drew her to him like a tiny insect to a bright light. Their hands touched as they were both helping themselves to ratatouille.

The tall man pulled back. "I'm sorry. Please go ahead."

Chantal blushed. "No, it was my fault. Shouldn't have charged ahead like that. But I'm starving and possibly a little drunk."

His hazel eyes crinkled as he smiled. "You're not the only one. The champagne tends to go to my head. And I'm afraid I've had quite a lot of it."

Chantal giggled. "Me too. I need to get some food to soak it all up."

He heaped her plate with food, topping it with a large slice of *pain de campagne*. "Here, this should help."

"Thank you, uh—?"

"Jean," he replied. "Jean Gardinier."

"*Bonjour,* Jean, I'm Chantal Bourcier."

"Beautiful, like your name." He finished piling food on his plate. "Now we need a place to sit down. Preferably away from this crowd. What do you say?"

Chantal was going to protest that she had to sit with the other bridesmaids and say she would see him after dinner, but when their eyes met, she found that the only thing she wanted to do was to be with him. Confused, she looked away. What was happening? She had never felt to so drawn to a man before. He was very handsome but she had met handsome men before. What was so special about Jean was his air of sophistication, the intelligence in his eyes and the way he looked at her with such intensity she felt she was the only person in the world of any importance to him. She didn't know anything about him—what he did for a living, or how old he was or even if he was married. But none of that mattered to her.

She smiled. "I think that would be wonderful."

They slowly wandered through the throng and found a place at the back of the garden, where an umbrella pine held its branches like shielding arms over a small, rusty, cast-iron table with two rickety chairs.

"Not part of the seating plan," Jean remarked. "But nobody will see us here."

Chantal glanced up at the terrace, where the wedding guests were taking their places at long tables covered in white tablecloths. Nobody noticed them or even looked around to see where she had gone. She turned to him. He had taken off the jacket of his beige linen suit and loosened his blue silk tie. With his brown hair tumbling over his forehead and the mischievous air in his eyes, he looked younger than earlier. She suddenly wanted to know all about him.

"Who are you?" she asked. "Why have we never met before?"

"Maybe we weren't meant to meet until now?"

Chantal nodded. "You're right. I probably wasn't ready." She picked up her fork. "Why don't I eat and you tell me about yourself?"

He laughed. "If you allow me to take a few bites now and then."

"Of course," Chantal muttered through a mouthful of chicken and ratatouille.

"And then I want to know all about you."

"That seems fair enough," Chantal agreed. "But you go first."

As Jean started telling her about himself, between bites of food, she felt she wanted to listen to his deep voice forever. He was eight years older than her and was involved in the property business. Born in Marseille, he moved to Nice with his family when he was a teenager and started working in his father's estate agency when he left college.

"Property," she said when she finally allowed him to take a break. "That sounds interesting. I'm doing a business degree at the moment, but I don't know what I'm going to do when I finish. I'm only twenty years old, so I have plenty of time to make up my mind. But I suppose you find me very immature."

He leaned across the table and plucked one of the flowers that had dropped from her hair and tucked it into his button hole. "I find you enchanting."

She met his eyes and knew in an instant she was in love.

After a brief, intense courtship, they were married in the garden of Les Temps Heureux, her parents' house in the hills above Cap d'Antibes and then spent their honeymoon sailing around the coast all the way to Italy. Jean set up the agency in Antibes, and after both her parents had died, they moved into the house on the hill where they were married.

Such happy times, Chantal thought wistfully. *Will they ever come back? Is selling the house a big mistake? But it has to be done. It might help to sever the links with the past. And the money will be a welcome boost to our economy.* She hoped Flora wouldn't do anything to ruin the chances.

Chapter 6

Flora hung up and hurried up the stairs. What was up there? She heard Ross walk around a room just off the landing, where the half-open door revealed dusty floorboards. He turned around as she came in.

"Nice room. It even has a balcony with great views. Could be a good master bedroom."

Flora looked around. "It's empty."

"What did you expect?"

"I don't know," she said, feeling flustered. She had to get him to go back downstairs. But how? Wouldn't it seem strange to view a house and not see all of it?

He moved past her, walked to the door of the adjoining room and opened it. "Bathroom. Great space. And the suite must be from the time when the house was built. Just look at these beautiful washbasins."

Curious, Flora followed him inside. The bathroom was huge, with twin porcelain washbasins shaped like giant seashells with ornate taps and a bath big enough for several people. The walls were covered with sea-green tiles, and the large window overlooked the beach and sea beyond.

"What a beautiful bathroom," she exclaimed. "How lovely to lie in the bath and look out at sea."

"Wonderful," Ross agreed and turned one of the taps. He jumped as water gushed into the washbasin. "Oops. I'd no idea the water was turned on. I didn't think anyone lived here."

"The house isn't occupied, as far as I know," Flora said.

"What about those towels, then?" Ross pointed at two white bath towels hanging from a hook beside the bath.

"Could have been left by the previous owner before they moved out."

"And this?" Ross picked up a bar of soap from the wash basing and sniffed it. "Magnolia. Lovely. By Guerlain, if I'm not mistaken."

"Strange." Flora moved to the door. "If you've seen enough, maybe we could go downstairs? We haven't seen the kitchen or the garden yet."

"I haven't seen all the rooms up here. One more to go—the one at the end of the corridor."

Flora backed out of the bathroom. "I'm sure it's the same as all the others."

He looked at her curiously. "Strange way to show a house. Don't your buyers usually want to see every nook and cranny before they make a decision?"

"Uh, yes, of course." Flora felt her face redden. "It's just that I thought—"

"What? Are you in a hurry? I could see the rest on my own and then drop the key back to the agency, if you have another appointment."

"No, I don't."

"Okay, then. Let's see that last room up here and then go down." He moved swiftly past her, walked down the corridor and pushed at the door. But it didn't open. He pushed at it again and rattled the handle. "It's locked."

Flora joined him and pushed at the handle. "You're right."

"Do you have a key?"

Flora pulled the key ring out of her bag and examined the keys. "These are only the keys to the gate, the front and back doors."

He looked deflated. "Oh. Okay. Maybe you can get the key for when I come back? I'll certainly want to see this house a second time before I make a decision."

"Of course." Flora felt herself sag with relief. "I'll speak to my boss, Chantal Gardinier. I'm sure she'll get the missing key and have the room opened when you come back next time."

"Perfect. Let's go see the rest of the mansion." He sprinted down the stairs ahead of her.

Flora trailed behind, casting another glance at the locked door. What was in that room that had to be hidden from view?

* * *

There was an eerie calm at the agency when Flora got back. Daisy was talking to an English couple at her desk, and Chantal was working at her computer in her office, the door half open to the main shop. She glanced up as Flora entered.

"Did you manage to keep him from going upstairs?" she enquired.

"No. He was already up there when you called. But there was nothing much there, except for a room that was locked. Ross—the client, I mean—asked to see the house again and to have the key to that room too."

"Of course. That can be arranged," Chantal replied and switched off her computer. "When does he want to see it?"

Flora took the keys from her bag and put them on Chantal's desk. "He's going to speak to an architect and will be in touch. I think he'll want to do some repairs and alterations."

Chantal stiffened. "Alterations? What kind of alterations?"

"He wants to build a proper terrace at the back and knock out part of the back wall to build on a bigger kitchen."

Chantal looked at her blankly. "Oh. Did you tell him about the increase?"

"Yes. He said he'd speak to his bank."

Chantal nodded. "Good. That means he'll probably buy the property."

"For two million? Just like that? What does he do that earns him so much money?"

Chantal smiled. "What does he do? Nothing. Absolutely nothing."

"How's that possible?"

"I don't really know much about him. Just that he's very wealthy."

"But Ross looks so…so…"

"Normal?"

Flora nodded. "Yes. Like a college student or a maths teacher on holiday or something. Not at all like someone who's very rich. I thought he was a bit of a nerd, really. Very good-looking but in a wholesome way. And I'd never have thought he was wealthy."

"Maybe he tries not to show it? Trying to keep a low profile so he won't attract attention."

"I suppose."

Chantal gathered up her handbag, phone and keys and got up from her desk. "I have to go. I think Iris is coming back from her doctor's appointment soon, so the three of you will have to look after things for the rest of the day."

"Of course."

"There are two more showings today, but Daisy will tell you where they are. One of the houses is near La Tourette up in the hills, but you can borrow Iris's car. I take it you know how to drive?"

"Of course."

"The buyers are English. Retired couple looking for that place in the sun they've seen on TV. You have to sell them that dream. Do you think you can handle that?"

"I'll do my best."

"*Très bien.*" Chantal stood by the door and looked at Flora appraisingly. "I think you can handle a lot of things,

Flora McKenna. I have a feeling there's a lot more to you than that sweet and gentle exterior."

Chapter 7

Although it was only twenty-four kilometres from Antibes to the village of La Tourette-sur-Loup, it took Flora more than half an hour to get there in Iris's battered Renault. It was a nerve-wracking drive up a steep road with many hairpin bends.

The English couple, who would be looking at the house for sale just outside the village, fell silent while Flora struggled with the bad road. Both in their early sixties, they didn't look like a very happy couple. Flora had a feeling they were in conflict with each other from the moment they stepped into the car. The wife, a chirpy blonde woman called Dotty, chatted nervously during the first part of the trip, telling Flora how much she loved Provence and how she had always dreamed she would live there. The husband, a dour man with a pinched face, looking uncomfortable in his Ralph Lauren polo shirt and white shorts, didn't join in his wife's enthusiastic chatter. He looked out the window with a blank expression, as if he just wanted the pain to be over.

Flora finally came to a stone wall with an entrance not wide enough for the car. She pulled up.

"I think we have to walk the rest of the way. The house is down that track. Only two minutes or so," she said, hoping she was right.

They got out of the car into the blinding sun and searing heat. Flora put on her sunglasses and looked around. The vegetation consisted of scruffy, gnarled cork oaks and small olive trees climbing up a terraced garden devoid of grass or flowers. The noise of the cricket was deafening up there in the hills. The small house stood on a knoll above them, overlooking the valley and the mountains beyond. The sea glinted in the far distance. On closer inspection, Flora realised it was a near ruin and bore little resemblance to the charming cottage depicted in the brochure.

"It's a little rustic," she said. "But look at the views. Amazing, don't you think?"

"Rustic," the husband jeered. "You mean wrecked, don't you?"

"But Peter, just look at the roses climbing over that wall," Dotty chortled. "And the lovely shutters and the well. Look, it's got a bucket hanging over it."

"The shutters are falling off and the well's probably dry."

"But that terrace is enchanting." She hurried up to the house and stood on the terrace, closing her eyes to the sun. "The view's even better from up here," she called.

"The view," Peter scoffed. "And the roses. That's all she sees." He turned and looked to the other side of the garden. "What about that eyesore, then?"

Flora turned and saw a rusty iron shed. "It belongs to the farm next door." She picked up the brochure. "The adjoining farm will supply goat's cheese and olive oil at a very reasonable price. The fruit trees will yield a good crop of apricots and peaches in the summer months," she read.

"How lovely," Dotty chanted from the terrace. There was a sudden crash followed by a yelp.

"What happened?" Flora exclaimed and ran up to the terrace, where Dotty was scrambling to get up among broken timbers. "Dotty? Are you okay?"

"I'm all right," she panted. "It was the railing that kind of came apart when I leant on it. No problem. Easy to fix."

Her husband, who had walked more slowly up the slope,

put his hand under his wife's elbow and helped her up. "Has this convinced you that it's not the house for us?"

Dotty brushed dust and splinters off her peasant skirt. "We haven't seen the inside of the house yet. It might be a true gem."

Peter sighed. "I doubt it. But let's get it over, then. If you would be so kind as to unlock the door, Flora."

"Of course." Flora got out the keys and unlocked the door, which opened with a loud creak. "After you," she said and stepped back, letting Dotty and Peter go inside ahead of her.

The interior of the house was a lot better than the exterior. Although much of it was in a very poor state of repair, the living room with its fireplace and exposed beams had an old-fashioned, cosy charm that was hard to resist. The farmhouse kitchen and the three bedrooms had an equally appealing shabby-chic atmosphere, and Flora found herself quite enchanted by this little house. She could tell Dotty was completely bowled over. But Peter was not.

At the end of the tour, when they were again standing on the terrace, Flora noticed Dotty had tears in her eyes.

"I just want to stand here for a while," she said. "Just to look at the view and smell the roses and say goodbye to this dear little house." She looked past her husband at Flora. "I have this little sadness, you see. This tiny pain in my heart. I've had it for quite some time. When I came here, I felt—" She stopped, looking embarrassed. "Silly, I know, but that's feelings for you." She made a movement as if to shake herself. "Houses," she said, "have vibes. Happy or sad. This is a happy house. It'll make whomever lives here feel content and calm. I know it's a wreck, Peter, and I know you don't want to take it on. So we'll leave it and look for something else, something more practical. But just let me stand here on my own for a minute."

Flora moved away and walked down the steps to the

lower part of the garden to give Dotty the private movement she obviously needed. Hearing footsteps behind her, she turned and discovered Peter following her.

"I just want to give her some time alone," Flora said. "She's obviously sad about something."

"Yes. She lost her sister a while back. They were very close. That's why she wanted to move away."

"But you don't?"

"No. I don't see the point. I'd like to find a place near Nice. An apartment we could let during the summer months."

"But I thought you said in your emails to us you wanted something rural?"

Peter's eyes hardened. "I don't remember what we said. In any case, I think it's dishonest of you to make up a brochure with pictures that are far removed from reality." He made a gesture with his hand towards the house. "That house needs a lot of work before it's habitable. What's the point of telling lies when it will all be revealed when you show the house?"

Flora bristled, although she knew he was right. "That's not my fault. I work at the agency. I don't run it."

"So you take no responsibility for the dishonest way they operate?"

"Well… I…" Flora found herself stuck for words. "It's very difficult."

"I'd find it impossible. But of course, unlike you, I have standards. I suppose if I asked you if it's going to be possible to get electricity up here, you'd say there'd be no problem? And that planning permission for a swimming pool would be a breeze?"

"Uh…" Flora paused. "Okay, I suppose I would. But you're right. The agency does operate in a way that's not exactly morally correct. But what can I do about it? All the agencies around here do the same."

"I suppose. Not a nice business to be in. But moral standards are a luxury few can afford." He looked up at the house, where his wife was still looking at the view. As he stood there, Flora was astonished to see his face soften. "She would be very happy here."

"Looks that way, yes."

He turned back to Flora. "I'd buy the house subject to planning permission. But you'd have to knock at least a hundred thousand off the price. as well."

"That's a big price cut," Flora protested. "And they don't do that here. Subject to planning, I mean."

"About time they started. Wouldn't the agency benefit if it was known to be more buyer-friendly than any of the others? More honest in its sales tactics? If your brochures showed pictures of the houses the way they really are instead of these glamour shots that all look like some kind of scam when the buyers see the reality?"

Flora looked at him while she thought. He was right, of course, and his words sparked an idea in her mind. An honest agency? Could there be such a thing in the south of France, where most of their business was selling dreams to people with unrealistic expectations? Why not? It would take time and could mean a loss of business for a while. But in the long run…she smiled.

"Thank you," she said. "You might just have given me an idea that could cost me my job."

He smiled broadly, transforming his sour face. "And you have sold me a house that will probably ruin me."

* * *

Hot and tired, Flora shuffled into the office and threw her bag on her desk. It had been encouraging to talk to Peter and Dotty, during the long drive back, about their plans for the house and all the renovations they would do. Flora was also thinking about the idea Peter had given her. An honest, more ethical agency? How could she sell it to Chantal? But she would say no. Forget it. An impossible notion.

Her phone rang. She frowned and picked it up. Who could that be? The caller id didn't show a number she recognised. More bad news, probably. She answered on the fourth ring.

"Hello?"

"*Bonsoir*, Flora. This is Philippe Belcourt."

Her heart suddenly skipped a beat. "Oh, uh, bonsoir."

"Hard day?"

"Very."

"Sorry to hear that. I'm calling to ask if you're free to have dinner with me tonight. I could pick you up at the office."

Flora blinked. A date? With Philippe Belcourt? She caught sight of herself in the mirror by the door to the office. Her limp hair and her face shining with sweat were not exactly what she would have liked him to see. She needed a shower and shampoo urgently, not to mention make-up and a change of clothes. The green top, so fresh and cool that morning, stuck to her back and the linen trousers were wrinkly.

"Thank you. I'd love to, but maybe I should go home and change first," she croaked.

"No time. I've got a table at *La Colombe d'Or* for eight o'clock. That's in St Paul de Vence, if you haven't heard of it."

"*La Colombe d'Or*?" Flora stammered. "Of course I've heard of it."

"In that case, you'll understand I can't change the booking."

"Of course," Flora replied, her head spinning. Why did he suddenly want to take her out to dinner? He hadn't seemed that keen the last time they met and had practically thrown her and her suitcase out of the car. "But will I have time to change?"

"No. It takes a good half hour to get there from Antibes."

"But it's only—" She looked at her watch. "Shit, it's quarter past seven," she blurted out. "I had no idea it was that late."

"Exactly. I'll be there in fifteen minutes."

"Oh, uh…" Flora said, a wave of panic making her heart race. But he had hung up. She stared at Daisy, who had been listening intently. "That was Philippe Belcourt."

"The sexy photographer?"

"Yes. He'll be here…oh God, I'm a mess."

"What, what?" Daisy shouted. "He's taking you to *La Colombe D'Or*?"

"Yes! And he'll be here in fifteen minutes and I look like shit," Flora moaned.

Daisy shot up from her chair. "We'll soon fix that."

"How?" Flora wailed, tearing at her hair.

Daisy looked at her watch. "Fourteen minutes left. Let's get going. Go into the staff toilet. There are towels and wash-cloths in the small cupboard over the sink. Use the soap and wash what you can. I have some dry shampoo in my bag. I'll use that and do your hair. What about make-up?"

"What about it? I have some mascara and lipstick, and I think I might have a tinted moisturiser, too. But my clothes—"

"Okay, okay," Daisy interrupted. "Go and do as I say and we'll fix the rest later. I'll pop into the boutique across the road and get something for you. They're still open and I know the owner. Twelve minutes to go."

"This is mad," Flora complained, but she went into the staff toilet, stripped off her top and started to wash herself with a facecloth she found in the cupboard. After removing her make-up, she spritzed on some eau de cologne just as Daisy knocked on the door.

"Are you ready? Nine minutes to go."

Flora opened the door. "Here I am. All clean at least."

Daisy squashed in beside her, waving a cream silk shift dress. "Look what I got! It was on sale, too. Only fifty euros, reduced from a hundred and fifty. I guessed your size would be a thirty-eight. Am I right?"

"I'm a twelve, whatever that is in France."

"No idea. Hop into it, anyway, and I'll do your hair while you slap some make-up on." She glanced at her watch. "Five minutes."

Flora wriggled into the dress while Daisy sprayed a little dry shampoo into her hair. While she brushed it out, Flora applied mascara, tinted moisturiser and blusher.

Daisy stepped back. "Two minutes to go and look at you!"

Flora turned to the mirror and stared at herself. "It's a miracle. I look human." She looked more than that, she realised as she kept looking. The dress, although slightly too snug, revealed her curvy figure and round breasts. Her hair had lost its limpness and looked clean and shiny and her cheeks were pink from the panic and excitement. "You're a genius, Daisy!"

Daisy blew on her nails. "I know. I had good material. But, hey, he'll be here soon."

She was right. They could see Philippe's car pull up outside just as they came out of the staff toilet.

"I hope he puts the top up, or your hair will be all messy again," Daisy said. "He's getting out. Gee, he looks nice. For an old guy," she added.

"For any guy," Flora mumbled as she watched Philippe walk up the door of the agency.

He smiled broadly when he saw her and held the door open. "You look adorable, Flora. I don't know what you were fussing about earlier."

"Thank you," was all Flora managed as she looked into his brown eyes.

Daisy winked and made a thumbs-up behind Philippe's back. "Have a good time," she called as they left.

* * *

When Chantal got home, she found the apartment in darkness. Jean must have gone to sleep in front of the evening news again. She hadn't meant to get home that late, but she went shopping and then bumped into an old school friend who asked her to have a drink and then they had started chatting, gossiping viciously about former classmates. She simply forgot what time it was until her friend announced she had to rush on to a dinner party. Realising it was past eight o'clock and Jean would be both hungry and anxious, she half ran up the hill from the centre of Antibes to their apartment on the top floor of a tall building.

"Jean?" she called while running from room to room opening shutters and flinging windows open to let in the cool evening breeze from the sea. "I'm home, Jean. Where are you?" But her words were met with silence.

In the bedroom, the bed was messy, as if Jean had just got up, and his pyjamas lay in a heap on the floor. But no evening news. The blank screen stared back at her, telling her nothing. She looked wildly around, looking for clues, but there were none. Then the doorbell rang. Was it Jean? She ran to the door and wrenched it open, ready to scold him for going out on his own. But it was the young woman who lived in the adjoining apartment, standing there looking at Chantal as if she was trying to soften the blow of some very bad news.

"Chantal," she said. "Jean—"

"What?" Chantal demanded. "Where's Jean? If you know where he is, please tell me!"

"He's in hospital," the young woman said and put her hand on Chantal's arm. "He…he fell down the stairs and hit his head."

Chantal stared at her. "The stairs? But why didn't he take the lift? Why did he walk down five flights of stairs?"

"He wasn't walking down—he was on his way up. He laughed when I got into the lift with the baby buggy and said he wanted some exercise. He needed to get fit, he said. It would be easier for you if he was stronger." The young woman's eyes filled with tears. "So brave. But anyway, he hadn't gone up more than one flight when I saw him topple over and fall. When the lift reached our floor, I got out and called my husband who rushed down and saw Jean lying there, unconscious. So we called an ambulance. It arrived within ten minutes, and they took him to the Centre Hospitalier in Antibes."

"Oh." Chantal looked blankly at the woman. "When was this?"

"About half an hour ago. We rang your agency but only got the voicemail. Then we tried your mobile, but there was no reply, so we left a message."

"I didn't hear it. So much noisy traffic."

"I know." The young woman glanced back at the open door of her apartment from where the wailing of a baby could be heard. "I have to go back. The baby—"

"Of course. Go and look after your baby. I have to go to the hospital."

"I hope the news won't be too bad."

"So do I," Chantal said with feeling.

But the news couldn't have been worse.

"A stroke," the doctor said when Chantal arrived at the emergency ward.

Chantal burst into tears. "No! Please tell me it's not true. Where is he? Can I see him?"

"He's not here. We transferred him immediately by helicopter to the stroke unit at the St Roche hospital in Nice, where he can be assessed and get the best care."

Chantal tried to calm down. "Thank you. That's the best option, isn't it?"

"It's the only option," the doctor said.

"But how bad is it? Could you tell?"

"Not really. He was unconscious and came to briefly. But we put him under sedation to keep him calm for the journey. The stroke unit in Nice will be able to tell you more."

Chantal nodded. "Of course. I'll get over there right away."

The doctor put his hand on her shoulder. "It's not going to be easy. The recovery is long and hard. Your husband is going to need your support."

"I know," Chantal said. "I'll have to put my life on hold for a while."

"For the rest of his life, perhaps," the doctor said. "However long that will be."

Chapter 8

La Colombe d'Or, situated at the entrance of the quaint hilltop village of St Paul de Vence, looked little more than an old farmhouse from the outside. Inside, Flora gazed at paintings of famous artists, such as Picasso, Matisse, Chagall and many more on the whitewashed walls. The tall windows were open to the garden, and there was a delicious smell of food. Their table was ready. As Flora followed the waiter, she noticed several famous faces among the guests, most of them French. There was a low murmur in the dining room as if the guests were telling each other secrets, and many of them glanced up as Flora and Philippe weaved their way through the dining room to their table beside one of the open windows.

The waiter pulled out a chair. "Please, Mademoiselle," he said and flicked a starched linen napkin into Flora's lap.

Philippe sat down opposite, beamed at her and opened the very large and colourful menu. "So, what would you like for a starter?" he asked.

Overwhelmed with the vast array of dishes, Flora searched for something she recognised. But the list of hors d'oeuvres was too long and complicated.

"I don't know," she mumbled. "Why don't you choose?"

"Better than that." Philippe flicked his fingers, and the waiter reappeared at their table instantly. "Xavier, could you please take us through the menu?"

"Certainly," Xavier said in that lilting formality some Frenchmen used when speaking English that Flora always found so amusing. It sounded to her as if they were negotiating a contract. "If you will excuse me for my English," he said. "At first, we have the artichokes with its vinaigrette of raspberry vinegar and olive oil. Then we have langoustines with a delicate rouille and salade frisée." And on and on he went. By the time he had come to the end of the main courses, Flora's stomach was rumbling loudly.

"I'll have the langoustines," she said, interrupting his flow, "and the fillet mignon with pommes duchesse, medium rare, please."

"You have made a very good choice," Xavier said and wrote her order on his notepad. "And Monsieur? What does he wish?"

Philippe rattled off his order in French and then picked up the wine list. He scanned it quickly and ordered a glass of Chablis for Flora to go with the langoustines and a glass of St Emilion, premier cru, for them each to follow.

"I'm having the foie gras, followed by lamb. Only one glass of wine for me. I'm driving, so I have to be careful, I'm afraid."

Flora nodded. "Of course."

"But if you want more wine, I'll order a bottle for you."

"God, no," Flora protested. "I don't have a good head for wine. I'm the original cheap date. Two glasses and I'm anybody's."

Philippe laughed. "Sounds promising."

"Not really. I know when to stop. Except if I'm feeling reckless."

Philippe waggled his eyebrows. "Let me know when that happens."

"I'll send you an email."

He put his hand on hers and leant forward, looking deep into her eyes. "I hope I'll be close enough for you to whisper it in my ear."

They were interrupted by Xavier placing a large glass of cold white wine in front of Flora. "Your wine, Mademoiselle." He placed a basket of bread and a small pot of herb butter on the table. Another waiter served them chilled water and a plate of olives.

While they nibbled on the bread and olives, Flora looked around the dining room at the other guests. Spotting a very famous face, she leaned closer to Philippe. "Don't look now, but have you seen who's at the table under the big Matisse?"

Philippe glanced over her shoulder. "Yes. I think they're hoping to stay incognito. Let's pretend we haven't seen them. Or better still, that we have no idea who they are."

"I didn't know they were having an affair," Flora whispered. "I thought she was married."

He nodded. "She is. But I have a feeling it's about to end."

"How sad," Flora said. "I suppose that's what happens when two very attractive people make a movie together. The chemistry between them when they're acting spills over into their real lives."

"I'm sure it does."

Their starters were served with great flourish by two waiters. Flora fell on her food, and Philippe watched her with obvious amusement as she stuffed langoustines, salad and bread into her mouth.

"Shorree," she mumbled through lettuce leaves and raspberry vinaigrette, "but I didn't have time for lunch."

"Hard day?" His eyes were sympathetic.

Flora nodded. "This job is a lot more stressful than I thought it would be."

He put down his fork. "How so?"

Flora sighed and looked into the distance. Should she tell him how she felt about having to tell lies in order to sell a house? His eyes were so kind and he seemed genuinely interested.

"It's difficult to explain," she said. "But, for example, today

I showed this wreck of a house to a couple who are hoping to move here and spend their retirement in a sunny climate. Of course, the photo in the brochure made the house look romantic and cosy. But in reality—"

"It's a ruin?" he filled in.

Flora nodded and took a bite from a langoustine. "Lovely place. Could be done up to be really gorgeous. But it has no water or electricity, and there's this ugly shed next door. None of which was mentioned in the glossy brochure. I was really embarrassed."

"So what happened?"

"The husband was really annoyed and told me off. But in the end, he seemed interested in the house provided he can get it for a hundred thousand less and on the condition they get planning permission for the renovations. Which, of course, is impossible. I haven't met the mayor yet. Dealing with him is Chantal's job. I have a feeling it's tricky."

"Your boss is very resourceful. She can cope with the mayor's office."

Flora stopped eating. "You know her?"

He nodded. "Yes. We've known each other a long time. I did some photo shots for her. I suspect I might have done the photos of that house you were showing today. Old farmhouse near Tourette sur Loup?"

"That's right," Flora exclaimed. "You took those photos?"

He looked slightly embarrassed. "Yes. I'm afraid I did."

"Great job. You made the house look like Snow White's cottage. I must say, seeing the real thing was a bit of a disappointment."

"I know. I told Chantal at the time. But she insisted it would be a great lure. It would make people want to see it, she said. And then, they'd be so blown away by the setting, they'd want to buy it despite the state of it. It hasn't happened yet, of course." He shrugged and took a piece of bread from the basket.

"No. And it probably won't. But—" She stopped. Telling him her idea probably wasn't a good move. It wouldn't ever be possible anyway.

"But—?"

"Oh, nothing."

He didn't reply but looked over her shoulder with sudden interest. She turned her head to see what he was looking at. The couple behind them were holding hands and then the man leaned forward to kiss his companion. Flora turned back, wanting to give them some privacy, and noticed Philippe was doing something with his phone.

"Do you need to call someone?" she asked.

He put down the phone. "No. Just checking for messages."

She studied him for a moment. His elegant way of dressing, his sleek good looks and charming smile hid something she couldn't quite decipher. He wasn't all he appeared, she realised and wondered if she would ever find the real Philippe under the smooth surface. But for now, she didn't care. She was enjoying the evening, the fancy dinner and the admiring glances of a very handsome man.

Their plates were removed and replaced with their main course. Another waiter arrived with two glasses of red wine. They ate in silence for a moment, Flora savouring the wonderful flavours of the meat in its red wine and herb sauce.

"Good?" Philippe enquired.

"Mmm, yes," Flora mumbled through her mouthful.

"Worth the trip?"

"Of course, you rogue."

"Glad to hear it. But enough about me. Let's roll the film back to the beginning. What were you saying?"

"What?"

"You started to say something a moment ago. Something about the agency. You said 'but', and I felt you had something on your mind, something important."

Her reticence softened by wine and food, Flora started to tell him about her idea.

"I was thinking," she said, "that if the agency changed its policy somehow and presented a more honest image, it might be good for business. I mean, if the photos in the brochures and on the website were more realistic and the prices lowered, maybe all those houses that have been on our books for years might get sold. And maybe, if we built up a reputation for not being as dishonest as most of the other agencies—" She stopped. "I'm not sure I'm explaining this properly."

He poured water into her glass. "Yes, you are. I know what you mean. And it's not a bad idea. Except you'll never get it past Chantal."

"I know." Flora sighed. "It's just a dream, really."

"It's good to have dreams." He looked over her shoulder again. Then back at her with a sudden intensity that made her face feel hot. There was something about him that affected her more deeply than she cared to admit. He was so much older than her, at least ten years, but despite that, he disturbed her sexually like no other man. He had only ever give her two polite kisses on the cheek, touched her hand or brushed her bare shoulder when he helped her with the seat belt in the car, but even that slight touch had sent shivers down her spine and made her tingle all over. Did he feel the same attraction? She met his eyes and thought she saw something there, a hint of laughter mingled with something else, something sensual and perhaps a little dangerous.

Xavier materialised before them. "How is the meal progressing?" he asked. "Is everything to your satisfaction?"

Flora giggled.

Philippe put his hand on her arm. "Yes," he said without taking his eyes off her, "I would say it's progressing very much to our satisfaction."

* * *

Chantal sat by the bed, looking at Jean's inert form. He was breathing evenly with the help of the oxygen tube in his nose. He looked so peaceful and calm lying there, nearly as if...no. She pushed the thought away from her mind. She didn't wish him dead, she wished him recovered, alive, talking to her, even if it didn't make much sense anymore. Although life with him was no longer that of a husband and wife, she loved him still and wanted to care for him, almost like a mother for her child.

Her liaison with a younger man, who adored her body and worshipped her mind, didn't make her feel guilty. Jean didn't know about it, and even if he had known, he wouldn't have understood its implications. Her lover made her feel alive, and it helped her cope with Jean and with running the agency, which had been so enjoyable at first, but was now more like a painful duty. But the bills had to be paid and the cost of living was rising, so the money had to come from somewhere. The sale of the house, her childhood home and her bolthole for the past few years, would bring in much needed money, too. She sighed, wondering where she would meet her lover now. His studio was out of the question, as he was so well known all over the Riviera. They had to find somewhere, away from prying eyes and wagging tongues. Gabriel, her angel of mercy, as she called him for fun, might come up with an idea. Or maybe one of those old houses lingering in the hills, unsold and unloved, would provide a temporary refuge and meeting place.

The door opened to admit a doctor in scrubs, his stethoscope around his neck. "Madame Gardinier? I'm Doctor Christian, the neurologist. If you have a moment, I need to talk to you."

Chantal stood up. "Yes, of course."

He moved aside to let her pass. "We can talk in the nurse's treatment room."

Chantal entered the small room that smelled strongly of

disinfectant, the doctor following behind her. He closed the door. "I wanted to talk about what we discovered during the CAT scan of your husband's brain."

Chantal shivered and pulled her cardigan tighter around her. "Yes?"

"He's had a brain haemorrhage, as we suspected. While it's serious, it's not life-threatening. And there's a good chance he'll recover to nearly ninety-five percent of what he was before with rest and rehabilitation. But it will take time and patience."

Chantal nodded. "Of course. I'll do everything I can to help restore him to—" She stopped. "I was going to say full health but that's not possible. But if he can get back to nearly the same as what he was, I suppose that's good news, no?"

"Yes. But there's more." The doctor looked at her as if assessing her mood. "We discovered something that could be positive. Something that might even get him back to what he was before he became so confused."

Chantal looked at the doctor. "What do you mean?"

He pulled out a chair. "Please, Madame, sit down."

Chantal sank down on the chair, her legs suddenly weak. What was he going to tell her? He looked even more serious than before, but his words had hinted at good news, not bad.

"I'm sitting," she snapped. "Please stop treating me like a child and tell me what you found."

"Of course." He leaned against the trolley and folded his arms. "What we found on the scan was a small tumour at the frontal lobe of the brain."

Chantal clapped her hand to her mouth. "A tumour?"

He nodded. "It's not as serious as it sounds. In fact, it could be good news, not bad. We think—at least the neurosurgeon and I do—that this is the cause of your husband's confusion and dementia."

"But he was diagnosed with early dementia three years ago."

"I know. But I don't think it was correct. I think this tumour's been there and has possibly been growing since then. This would have seriously affected his mood and his memory and even cognitive thinking."

Chantal stared at him, unable to find anything to say. "Go on," she mumbled.

"This type of tumour's often benign and completely operable. In fact, there's a new technique where the tumour's removed through the patient's nose rather than cutting open the skull."

"Oh God," Chantal mumbled. "I feel sick."

"Shall I get you a glass of water?"

She swallowed. "Please," she whispered.

"Just a moment." He went to the sink and filled a paper cup with water and handed it to her.

Chantal sipped the water, feeling slightly better. "Go on," she croaked.

"I won't go into more medical detail," the doctor said. "But I want you to know that, even if it's going to take time, we have reason to think your husband will, after the operation and quite a long recovery period, return to his old self."

Chantal couldn't believe it. What had he just said? That Jean would be... "He'll be well again?" she asked in a shaky voice. "The way he was? Before the onset of the dementia?"

The doctor nodded. "Yes. But it's a very long road back."

"I understand that."

"We can't operate until he's recovered from the stroke. And that could take over two months or more."

"I see."

"You'll have to spend a lot of time with him."

"Of course." Chantal threw the paper cup into the waste paper bin. "I'll do anything."

"Good. It will mean sitting by his bed for most of the day during the first few weeks. Talking to him, encouraging him, making him drink and eat and move."

"I don't mind," she said automatically while secretly flinching at the thought of sitting by a hospital bed all day every day for weeks. But what else could she do?

The doctor's voice cut into her thoughts. "The sooner we get him up and about again, the sooner we can deal with the tumour before it gets any bigger, you see. I understand you run some kind of business. I hope you can take some time off?"

"Time off?" Chantal said, wondering how that would be possible. The agency would go bankrupt in a week if she left it to one of those silly girls. Except…

"I might have a solution," she said as if to herself.

"A solution?" the doctor asked.

"Yes." Chantal nodded, knowing it was a gamble. But she had a feeling.

"Flora," she said. "She's the solution."

Chapter 9

They walked out of the restaurant into the warm velvety darkness. Stars glimmered in the ink-black sky, and the hint of a breeze cooled Flora's face. Without speaking, Philippe put his arm around her waist and drew her close.

"Flora," he whispered in her ear and kissed her lightly on the lips.

She could hear people leaving the restaurant behind them, talking, laughing, getting into cars. She pulled away but not before she returning his light kiss. "Thank you for a lovely dinner."

"Thank you for coming out with me tonight." His hand was warm on her waist, his mouth tickled her ear and his breath was hot on her face. When they were further away and walking along the ramparts, where they could see the lights of Nice edging the bay like a glittering diamond necklace, he stopped and pulled her close again.

"Thank you for coming out with me tonight." He touched her neck with his lips and ran his hands down her hips, cupping her buttocks. "Ma belle Flora," he said, pulling her tightly against him. "I have a house further up the hill. I'd like you to see it. But only if you want to. If you say no, I'll understand completely and take you home."

Flora laughed, her mouth against his neck. "And if I say yes, will you still respect me?"

"Of course."

As he pressed her closer still, she could feel he was aroused, and she responded by wiggling her hips and pressing herself even closer.

"I don't want you to respect me," she whispered. His body was taut and toned, his arms strong, and he smelled of lavender soap and newly ironed linen. Throwing caution to the soft breeze and forgetting everything about playing hard to get, she responded to his deep kiss with equal heat.

He pulled away and took her hand. Laughing, they ran to his car and jumped in. Philippe revved the engine and drove at breakneck speed up the hill until he came to a stop outside tall gates. He took out a remote and pressed it. The gates slid open and they drove in through a row of cypress trees. Flora could see a white one-storey building at the end of the drive with big windows overlooking the valley and the sea far below. A lone light glinted through the picture window behind the terrace.

"I left the light on," Philippe said as he switched off the engine. "I always do. Much nicer to come home to than a dark house."

"Beautiful house," Flora said, slightly awestruck.

"I love it." He took her hand. "Viens, ma chére, to my home and my bed."

"Yes," Flora breathed. "Your bed."

They didn't make it that far, however. Walking across the terrace, Philippe stopped and kissed her, undoing the tiny hooks at the front of her dress. Flora started unbuttoning his shirt, running her hands over his smooth chest. She shivered as he opened her dress and slid his hands around her to undo her bra. Her naked breasts against his skin ignited a flame that took them both by surprise. They stopped and sank down on a lounger at the edge of the terrace. Flora wriggled out of her dress and underwear, hearing him slide out of his trousers. Naked, she pulled him on top of her, opening her legs, her body melting into his. Moments later, they climaxed at the same time, perfectly synchronised in a crescendo of moans and cries.

Then they were still, breathing hard, smiling at each other through the darkness in a silent conspiracy.

"Love your bed," Flora mumbled.

"Sorry. I just couldn't wait," he whispered into her hair.

"Thanks for having me."

"You're welcome." He touched her face. "I didn't dare dream this would happen. I felt it would from the start but not so soon."

"I'm a hussy," she laughed. "Third time we meet and we're already having sex."

"Nothing wrong with that." He stood up. "Let's have a shower. There's one here, beside the pool."

"Good idea." Flora padded after him in the dim light of the moon that had just risen above the umbrella pines. Further away, she could see the pool and the little pool house beside it, where Philippe had already turned on the shower. She stepped in beside him and enjoyed the warm water cascading over them.

He ran soapy hands over her body. "You have such lovely creamy skin, Flora."

"Lily white, though. I have to be careful with the sun."

"That's a good thing."

"How would you feel if someone took a photo of us right now and sold it to some sleazy tabloid?"

"I would be proud to show what a beautiful woman I was with."

Flora pushed him. "You're horrible." Dripping, she got out of the shower and walked to the edge of the pool.

"Do you want to swim?" Philippe asked, drying his hair with a towel.

"I'd love to."

"Get in and float around. I'll go and get us some champagne."

"Perfect."

Without hesitating, Flora swung her legs over the edge and got into the cool turquoise water, floating on her back, looking up at the myriad of stars in the black sky. This was heavenly. She didn't want it to end. What a magical evening. Maybe it was a dream? She still felt the afterglow of Philippe's embraces and that wonderful climax.

Who was he really? she asked herself as she floated there. What was behind that glamorous façade? Was he a crook? A rogue? She had a feeling there was a lot to Philippe that he didn't reveal at once. Maybe she shouldn't have succumbed to his charms so easily, but it felt so inevitable, as if it was meant to happen, as if he had been waiting for her all this time.

"Flora," Philippe called from the terrace. "Your phone rang."

"Let it ring," she said, still looking at the stars. "I'll call them back."

"I'm afraid I answered. It's Chantal, your boss."

"For God's sake, what does she want at this hour?" Flora clambered out of the pool, found a towel and wrapped it around her. Muttering to herself about Chantal and how inconsiderate it was to call people late at night, she climbed the few steps to the terrace and took the phone Philippe handed to her.

"Champagne," he mouthed, pointing to the house.

Flora nodded and put the phone to her ear. "Yes?"

"Flora?" Chantal said in a shrill voice. "Sorry to interrupt your evening. But I have something to put to you. A proposal."

"A proposal? At this hour?" Flora couldn't help saying.

"It's only eleven o'clock," Chantal snapped. "Hardly the middle of the night."

"Well, no, but—"

"Never mind that. Just listen, please. I'm at the hospital in

Nice because my husband's very ill. He had a stroke earlier today."

"Oh, no!" Flora exclaimed. "I'm so sorry. How awful."

"Yes, very unfortunate. And of course, I'll have to spend a lot of time here at the hospital for a while."

"Of course."

"So that'll mean I can't run the agency efficiently. No use just coming in now and then, is there?"

"I suppose not," Flora said, waiting for the inevitable.

"So, I'm appointing you manager. Temporarily, of course."

"I see." Flora sat down on the low terrace wall, clutching the towel. "Manager? For how long?"

"Well, it could be months."

"Months?" Flora echoed. She smiled at Philippe, who, dressed in a white towelling robe, kissed her bare shoulder and handed her a brimming glass of champagne.

"Yes. It could be until October at least."

"Oh God, that long?" Flora sipped champagne and tried to focus. How on earth could she run a French agency without any proper training? "What about Iris or Daisy? They've been here longer than me and know the ropes."

"No, no," Chantal snapped. "Neither of them are any use. But you…I have this feeling you would do a very good job. And in any case, didn't you run an estate agency in Dublin for a couple of years?"

"Yes, but that was different. I don't have a clue about the procedures here."

"They're just minor details. I'll email you instructions tomorrow. That's all settled then," Chantal said and hung up.

Slightly dizzy, Flora switched off her phone.

"What's going on?" Philippe asked.

Flora sighed. "Nothing much. Chantal's husband's had a stroke. She's going to have to nurse him for the next five months. So she's just made me manager of the agency. And I really don't have a clue about French property laws and procedures. Fabulous, don't you think?"

He sat down beside her. "But it is, you know. Really good news."

She peered at him in the dim light. "How do you mean?"

"But don't you see? Now you can do what you said you wanted. You can make that honest and true agency."

"What? Behind Chantal's back?"

"Of course, mon chou. What better opportunity will you get?"

Flora thought for a while. Then she couldn't help smiling, a slow, wicked smile. "Sneaky. But I like it."

* * *

After hanging up, Chantal returned to her husband's bedside. There was no change. He was lying there, breathing heavily through the oxygen mask, a drip stuck into his arm. She sat down on a chair beside the bed and took his hand.

"Jean, it's me, Chantal. I'm here and I'll stay beside you until you get better. And you will. I know you will. The doctors are very hopeful. And I believe them. You're fighter, Jean, and so am I. We'll get through this together."

As she spoke, she breathed in the air, thick with disinfectant and medicine, and wondered how she would survive the next days, weeks and months. She looked at Jean's peaceful face and tried to remember the good times, those times when they had been so in love. She was only twenty when they met, and had been mesmerised by his good looks and mature charm. Eight years older, he was already successful in his career as an estate agent, the manager of one of the more important agencies on the Riviera. He then started his own business in Antibes, which they had run together until he became ill. They had a charmed life in the early days; they weren't too worried that they hadn't had children and, as time wore on, told each other it wasn't meant to be, so they might as well just enjoy being together. And they did.

Chantal squeezed Jean's hand and remembered this was the man who had taken her to Paris when she was bored and booked them into the George V because 'a beautiful woman should be spoiled,' he said. He pulled her into Cartier's on Rue Faubourg St Honoré and bought her a diamond ring, just because it was her birthday, her thirty-first, she remembered. Then on to Yves St Laurent to buy a silk shirt and a pair of black trousers, continuing to the Hermès shop for a handbag and shoes at Charles Jourdan. Breathless, laughing, but slightly worried about the money he had spent, she begged him to stop or they would be ruined.

"No, no," he said. "We got a huge commission from the sale of that villa on the Cap, and what better way to spend it?"

She smiled at the memory. She still had the whole outfit in her wardrobe. Timeless and classy, none of the items he bought would ever go out of fashion, even after nearly thirty years. Twirling the diamond ring on her finger, she looked at him again. He hadn't moved or reacted to her voice or touch. The happy memories faded and were replaced by sad ones.

The past three years had been so difficult and heart-wrenching: watching an intelligent, charming man slowly lose his memory and his intellectual capacity, becoming like a child—her child, whom she had to look after. Then the violent temper tantrums when he hit her and threw crockery around the flat.

"Early dementia," the doctor had said and shook his head. "Family history, of course. Nothing much to do. I'll prescribe a tranquiliser and sleeping pills. The temper tantrums should ease off. But he'll need a lot of care."

She believed him, and the results of the brain scan confirmed the diagnosis. The nightmare began. Her happy life was over, replaced by the daily chore of going to work and spending evenings with this stranger who used to be her husband, her best friend, her lover. He was able to look after himself, do simple chores, so she could go to work and not worry too much about him. She spent the evenings, mostly alone as Jean, like a small child, went to bed early. Chantal found herself wondering how she could escape this dreary, sad existence. She couldn't leave him or have him admitted to an institution. Not yet, anyway. He was still well enough to live a fairly normal life, even if that life was devoid of any pleasures. Just as she started to feel she would go insane if she didn't find a way out, she met Gabriel.

* * *

The exhibition was held in a small gallery in Mougins, high in the hills above Nice. Chantal had been dragged there by a friend who insisted she needed a break and a little bit of culture. Reluctantly, she called Jean, told him that she would be a little late and that she had ordered pizza for him. He replied in his usual distant tone that it was fine and that he would go to bed all by himself, as if he was seven years old and looking for approval for being a good boy. Feeling guilt mixed with relief, Chantal hung up and decided the short break would be good for her. She needed adult conversation and something else to think about.

It was early spring, and the mimosa had just come out in bloom all over the hills. The clear blue skies and the rosy glow of the late-afternoon sun created a dreamy, hazy light as Chantal drove up the winding roads and parked just below the village. Her pencil skirt and high heels were not ideal for walking up steep slopes, but she wandered slowly along the narrow road, taking a shortcut up the steps to the centre of the medieval village with its cobbled alleys and ancient stone-faced buildings. She hadn't been there for a long time and now took special delight in this visit.

She forgot about Jean and the heartache of his slow

descent into dementia and began to enjoy herself, looking into quaint shops and smelling the delicious food that was being prepared in all the little restaurants along the main street. She decided to have something to eat after the exhibition if her friend was free to join her. Even if she wasn't, Chantal decided, a meal there would be wonderful. Maybe at that restaurant she had spotted with a terrace overlooking the hills?

She found the gallery in a side street off the main square. *Vernissage*, the poster outside said, under a photo of a beautiful landscape. Then the artist's name: Gabriel Sardou. Chantal had seen his name mentioned in the culture section of Le Figaro and knew he was a much respected Provençal landscape artist.

Chantal stepped inside the gallery and was at once captured by the paintings, the exquisite colours, the shapes and forms and the incredible light that was so special in Provence. Many artists had painted Provence but never like that, never with that intensity and soul.

Mesmerised, she walked from painting to painting, lost in the views of the hills, the sea and the occasional mellow stones of old buildings. The paintings had a wistful, melancholic quality, as if the artist was sad about the modernisation and urbanisation of a part of France he loved.

Someone touched her shoulder and kissed her cheek. "Chantal. So glad you came. Wonderful paintings, don't you think?"

Chantal turned to her friend. "*Bonsoir,* Marie. Thank you for telling me about this wonderful exhibition. It's…it's…I can't find words to express how it makes me feel."

"I know," Marie said. "These are true masterpieces. I'll leave you to see the rest. But I'd like you to join me and some friends for dinner afterwards. Very casual. We've booked a table at Le Coq Rouge, that little restaurant on the edge of the ramparts. And we've invited Gabriel to join us. He's over there…" She waved her hand toward the back of the gallery. "Talking to some art critics but he said he'd join us later, so you'll be able to meet him and tell him how much you liked his paintings. Please say you'll come."

Chantal looked to the back of the gallery, where a tall man was talking animatedly to a group of journalists with cameras and notebooks, his dark hair flopping into his eyes. He looked up briefly and their eyes met. Chantal felt a strange electricity charge through her. His charisma was powerful, even at a distance.

Later, she would reflect on their meeting and realise it was meant to happen. When he entered the restaurant after the vernissage was over and joined the small group, he sat down beside Chantal and looked at her as if he had waited to meet her all evening. He took her hand and kissed it.

"*Bonsoir,* pretty lady," he said in a slightly hoarse voice. "Where have you been all my life?"

Clichéd as it sounded, Chantal was nevertheless bowled over by his warmth and the laughter in his eyes. Not mocking her, just delighted to be in her company.

"Right here," she said. "Waiting."

Chapter 10

"Look who's on the front page," Daisy said the next morning, waving a copy of *Nice Matin*.

"Who?" Flora asked from the terrace.

"*Them*. Martine Villiers and Johnny Bradshaw. In a restaurant. Kissing. And she a married woman with kids. At *La Colombe d'Or*. Isn't that where you were last night? Did you see them?"

"What?" Flora snatched the newspaper from Daisy. It was true. There they were, at that table behind theirs. The photo could only have been taken from one spot. She stared at the photo. Blood drained from her face as she realised what had been going on: Philippe looking behind her back, fiddling with his phone all evening. The house, the car, the swimming pool all shouted money, and this was how he earned it.

"The bastard!" she sobbed and picked up her phone.

"Who?" Daisy demanded. "What's going on?"

Flora didn't reply but punched in a number. "You liar," she yelled when Philippe answered. "You pretended to take me out to dinner when all you wanted was to use me as a prop."

"What are you going on about?" Philippe asked, sounding both sleepy and confused. "I had a wonderful time with a beautiful woman. What's wrong with that?"

"No you weren't," Flora snarled. "You were taking photographs. Of *them*. They're on the first page of this morning's *Nice Matin*. I bet you got a lot of money for that shot. It's probably going viral all over the world as we speak."

"I hope it does," he said, his voice full of laughter. "How did you know it was me?"

"It just came to me," Flora said. "You're a paparazzo, aren't you? Taking photographs of famous people when they think they're safe, just having a good time."

"And what's wrong with that? It's not as if I'm poking a telephoto lens through their bathroom window, is it? Which I wouldn't, by the way."

"Oh, really? How do I know?" Flora said sarcastically. "And here I was, thinking you asked me out to dinner because you *liked* me. But I was only a prop for you so you could go there and pretend we were a couple out to dinner, having fun."

"I do like you."

"Gee, I'm flattered."

"Oh, please. Stop bitching. It's my job. A shot of those two together like this can fetch twenty thousand euros just for exposure across Europe. If I can sell it to the US, it could be ten times that."

"Do I get commission?"

"No, but you got an excellent dinner."

"Big deal."

He took a deep breath. "Flora, I admit that, initially, you served as a back-up. Nobody would think you were anything else but a most adorable date for the evening. That's why I asked you. But…" he paused and when he continued his voice changed, "what happened after that was not something I planned. And it was wonderful. I hope it was for you too."

"Yes," Flora mumbled. "It was. I was so happy. Until I saw this morning's paper and then I felt…I felt used."

"I'm sorry. And yes, I did use you. But then…what happened was something between the two of us. Something so sweet and wonderful. Can you forgive me?"

"No."

"*Allons, chérie.* I think you're overreacting. It was only a silly photo."

"Which will make you a lot of money."

"Hopefully, yes," Philippe said.

"And it might cause them a lot of trouble and pain. Not to mention her family. Do you ever consider such things?"

"Sometimes, yes. But in this case, they were in a very public place. Do you really think we were the only ones to notice them?"

"You were the only one taking pictures."

Philippe sighed. "I really don't think it was such a crime. They're obviously going out in public. It's their fault for not being more careful to keep their relationship secret, if that's what they're trying to do."

"Still, it's a huge invasion of privacy."

"Maybe." He cleared his throat. "And I was just about to call you and thank you for last night. And ask you if you'd like to come with me to St Tropez this weekend."

"Who is it this time? Royalty?" Flora snapped. "I'm not going to be your decoy ever again, so forget it."

He was silent for a while. "That wasn't part of the plan. I want to get to know you. But I see that you wouldn't want to continue what seemed so promising."

"You got it."

"Well, in that case, we should end this conversation."

"You bet." Flora hung up and burst into tears.

* * *

As she walked into the office later that morning, Flora was met by a cold stare from Iris. "So you're the boss, now?" she asked.

Flora stopped. "Just temporarily. Chantal asked me to help out while her husband's recovering."

"Could take months," Iris said. "Don't know why she appointed you when I have more experience and more contacts in the mayor's office."

"I know. That's what I told Chantal. But she insisted," Flora replied, resisting the temptation to tell Iris that Chantal had said she was too hostile and rude to be able to deal with the officials and that telling the mayor he was a fascist pig wasn't the way to go when negotiation planning permissions. "I think it's my experience with running an agency that made her ask me."

"Okay. In that case, I'll pass the latest angry client on to you. They just called. An Irish couple who bought a medieval tower in the hills above Grasse. They wanted to build a terrace at the top and went ahead, but the builders have been stopped by the mayor's office. It appears it's a listed building, which nobody told them. They'll call back in a few minutes, they said."

"Oh my God, what on earth will I tell them?"

Iris shrugged. "Well, you're the boss with all that experience. I'm sure you can think of a way out." She went back to her computer with a satisfied smirk.

The couple called just as Flora was sitting down at Chantal's desk. They took turns to shout insults about the agencies until Flora managed to get a word in.

"This happened before I joined this agency," she said. "I agree it wasn't very nice not to mention you couldn't make alterations to the structure."

"'Not nice'?" the man snarled. "It was a fucking disgrace! We were fooled into buying this tower on the assumption we could build on to it. When we asked that…that whatever her name is, she just said 'it's absolutely possible' and she'd fix it with the mayor. Then the mayor's office knew nothing about it when we mentioned this. This is fraud, you know. We could sue you."

Flora cleared her throat. "Well, that's one way of looking at it, I suppose."

"It's the only way!" the wife screeched. "You'll be sorry you did this, you crook."

Flora bristled. "Hang on a minute. It's not as if someone held a gun to your head, is it? And did you ever stop to think that a medieval building such as this would probably be listed? Whatever the agency told you, maybe you should have had the sense to realise that building onto the tower would be against the law. Not to mention that adding anything to a beautiful old building would be in very bad taste," she added, despite knowing it wouldn't go down too well.

There was a brief silence. "I'm going to get legal advice," the husband snapped. "You'll hear from our lawyers very soon."

"I'll look forward to it. At least they'll be polite," Flora said and hung up. She stared into space for a moment, not yet ready to tackle the pile of letters on the desk. Well, that went down well. The new face of the agency she had planned to reveal that very day was nowhere to be seen. But she would have to tackle the old sins first, of course. She turned her attention to the mail. But before she could read the first letter, the phone rang.

Flora picked up with a sigh. "Flora McKenna, how can I help you?"

"You can accept my offer of two million for the villa on the hill," a cheery voice said.

"Who's this? I don't appreciate this kind of joke so early in the morning."

"How quickly you forget," the man said. "We were up there together only a few days ago."

"We were?" Flora racked her brain. A few days ago? Who...? Then it dawned on her. "Ross," she said. "Ross Fitzgerald."

"Bingo!"

"Sorry. But…you were saying?"

"I want the house. That house. You know, the one we looked at together."

"You do?" Flora said, feeling stupid. "Even for that price?"

"For any price. I know it was there, waiting for me. I was meant have it. To live there and be happy." He sounded wistful as if he hadn't been happy for a long time.

"Okay." Flora paused. This was it. Her first opportunity to be honest. "There are a couple of things I should tell you before we proceed."

"I hear a touch of doom in your voice. Don't tell me the house has been sold."

"No. It's still for sale. But—" She took a deep breath. "You won't be able to build on to it. It's a listed building, you see. It's a great example of neo-classism, inspired by le Corbusier, who even designed parts of this building and—"

"Slow down," Ross laughed. "I know all that. I had a suspicion that would be the case even if what I was suggesting would add to the attraction, not take away from it. But, no big deal. It's a true gem as it is."

"There's damp in the basement and parts of the roof are in poor shape." Flora said. "You'll need to rewire the whole house, too."

"You don't want me to buy it?" he asked, sounding puzzled.

"Yes, but with your eyes open. Not with some kind of dream of the perfect house. That's our new policy."

"That's one weird agency you've got there."

Flora laughed and finally relaxed. "I know. But I'm hoping this new ethos will catch on."

"It'll be popular with buyers, I'm sure. But listen, one thing—I'd like to have another look around the house before I hand over the cash. I haven't been in that locked room yet, either."

"I'm sure we can arrange that."

"Great. How about later today? Around five o'clock?"

"Of course. I'll get someone to show you around and get that room opened up."

"Fantastic. See you then," Ross said and hung up.

* * *

As Chantal sat by Jean's bedside, she thought about Gabriel and the first few weeks of their acquaintance. They met casually at first, just for a cup of coffee, a glass of wine or a short stroll along the seafront, not touching or even holding hands. To Chantal, those first weeks were about two people connecting, sharing thoughts and ideas, being friends. He told her about his childhood in his native Arles and then moving to Paris, where he studied art. He moved back to Arles, where he took up painting, specialising in landscapes combined with abstract. She, in turn, shared memories of her childhood spent in the beautiful house on the hill in Cap d'Antibes, the middle daughter of a big family, now scattered all over the world.

He was ten years younger than her, but the age difference enhanced their friendship in an odd way. At first he seemed like a younger brother to her, but when he looked into her eyes with an intensity that made her shiver, she knew he was more than that. She was afraid to touch him, to even shake hands, because she knew it would move their relationship to a level she wasn't sure she could handle. But their attraction to each other was like a time bomb, a pressure cooker, a volcano on the verge of eruption. The question was not if, but when. She knew it would happen. She also knew it would break her heart.

Jean stirred. His hand tightened on hers. His eyelids fluttered. "Chantal?" he mumbled.

She stood up and leaned over him. "Yes, Jean. I'm here. You're in hospital. You had a fall."

"A fall," he slurred. "I don't remember." His eyes opened and focused briefly on her face. He tried to lift his hand but only managed to move it slightly.

"Don't try to move, chéri." Chantal smoothed his hair off his forehead. "You must rest and get better."

He muttered something she couldn't make out. Then he looked at her again. "Don't leave me," he begged in a barely audible whisper.

"I'll stay here by your side," she promised.

He didn't reply but closed his eyes and drifted back into sleep.

Chantal pressed the bell for the nurse.

Only moments later, she padded in. "What's the problem?"

"He woke up," Chantal said. "And he spoke to me. Just a few words and his speech was slurred. But he knew me."

The nurse nodded. "That's good." She went to Jean's side and checked his pulse. "He seems to be sleeping normally now. The doctor will be here shortly, on his rounds. You can speak to him then."

"Thank you." Chantal settled down on her chair again and looked at Jean's sleeping face. He was snoring gently, looking more comfortable. His words rang through Chantal's mind reminding her of the song by Jacques Brel: *Ne me quittes pas*. Don't leave me. Jean said it often and Gabriel loved that song. He often hummed it after making love, his arms wrapped around her. Two men, both dependent on her. One so damaged, the other so needy.

And the house…her house, where she spent so many happy years growing up, and then the time with Jean. When he became ill, they moved to an apartment which was easier to manage and closer to the agency. It had stayed empty until recently, when she decided to sell it. She hadn't expected to find a buyer so quickly. When she realised it was a distinct possibility the wealthy young man was interested, she raised the price in the vain hope the sale wouldn't go through. But he accepted and offered a little more than the asking price. She had no choice but to agree. Flora would have to close the sale. It was all ready to go. Except…Chantal suddenly remembered the locked room. Oh God, it had to be tidied up and all traces of what went on there removed. She fished her phone out of her handbag and dialled a number.

Jean stirred and muttered something.

Chantal glanced at him while she waited for a reply.

"Gabriel," she whispered when he answered. "I can't explain now but I can't see you for a while. I need you to do something for me."

* * *

"This," Ross said, looking at the view from the garden, then up at the house, "is the one thing I would give everything I have to own."

"I'm sure it won't come to that," Flora said. "I heard you're not exactly poor."

He turned to look at her. "Who told you?"

"Chantal, my boss."

"What else did she tell you?"

Flora shrugged. "Nothing much."

He nodded. "Nothing much to tell. She doesn't know who I am."

Flora looked at him. "You're famous? I've never seen you before."

"That's because I keep away from the press."

"Who are you, then?" Flora began to feel annoyed.

"Never mind. It's not important."

"Don't you trust me?"

"I trust nobody." He looked at her for a moment as if trying to decide if it would be safe to tell her. Then he started to speak very quickly. "Okay, then I'll tell you, if you promise to keep it to yourself."

"I swear. Scout's honour."

He nodded and took a deep breath. "This is going to sound like some corny story from Reader's Digest or something. But here goes…I won the money."

"You won it? How? Gambling?"

"No. I bought a lottery ticket a year ago. Just on a whim on my way home from work. Didn't think I'd win anything. But…" He breathed deeply. In and out. "I won the jackpot."

"How much?" Flora asked.

"Twenty million."

"Dollars?"

He nodded. "Yes."

"American or Canadian?"

"American. I was working in Boston. In McDonald's. Just for the summer. I don't know why I bought that ticket. I never gamble or even bet on anything. I was in this all-night sandwich bar and saw the lottery tickets for sale. So I just went, 'A ham sandwich, a coke, a Hershey bar and a lottery ticket.' Then she—the checkout girl, I mean—said what numbers do you want? I just made up the numbers on the spot. And," he swallowed noisily, his face pale, "I won."

Flora stared at him. "Oh my God. Jesus, Mary and Joseph. How amazing. How incredible." She shook her head. "Sorry, but I kind of imagined it happening to me and wondered how I'd feel. I don't know how I'd feel, actually. Changes your life, doesn't it?"

He nodded. "Sure does. Forever. Not sure if it's for the best, though. The press and TV were all over me when the story broke. So I had to run and hide for a while."

"I've never seen you in the gossip mags," Flora remarked.

"I know how to keep a low profile."

"You must be very good at that."

He nodded. "You bet. And I'd appreciate if you kept my purchase of this house very quiet."

"Of course."

"I'll hold you to that. I wouldn't like to see those slime balls sneaking around here," Ross said in a voice laced with venom.

"Who do you mean?" Flora asked, startled by the anger in his eyes.

"Photographers. Paparazzi or whatever they're called. I've managed to escape them so far."

"I'm sure they won't find you here," Flora said in an attempt to reassure him.

His face relaxed. "I know. And you wouldn't tell anyone, would you?"

"Of course not," Flora promised, thinking briefly of Philippe. Hopefully, he would never find Ross. How could he unless she told him?

"Of course not," Ross echoed. "Who could you tell?"

"Exactly. And you know," she continued, "although this house will cost you around two million euros, that's very modest for someone as wealthy as you."

He shrugged. "Yeah, they'd expect me to fork out a lot more than that on some huge pile in St Tropez. But that's not what I want." He looked up at the simple design of the façade again. "This is perfect. Just the right size if I find someone mad enough to marry me. But not too big if I end up living here alone." He turned and looked out over the vast expanse of sea and sky. "This view is unique. The house is like an eagle's nest, sitting here on the edge of the rock. " He sighed, looking happy. "I was looking for a forever house. I think I've finally found it."

"Where did you live before?"

"I've been on my boat moored in the marina in Cannes. Not a huge yacht or anything, just a motorboat with living quarters. An old thing made of mahogany, built in the nineteen forties…quite an antique, really. Her name's Marie-Louise after my mom. I've been all over the world with the old girl since I ran away from the media."

"Is that how you've escaped recognition for so long?"

He smiled ruefully. "Yeah, I guess so. But now I'm sure they've forgotten all about me. It's time to settle down, make friends and meet women. I'm kind of sick of my own company by now."

"A new beginning?"

He grinned. "Yeah, if you want to call it that. I'm beginning to feel excited about it."

"What made you come to France?"

"My mother was French. She loved this area. So I thought I'd be closer to her here, somehow. She died a few years ago. I still miss her."

"Of course you do," Flora said, saddened by the forlorn look in his eyes. "I'm sure you'll love it here. Maybe you should change your name so that nobody will know who you are?"

"Nah. Don't feel like doing that. I like my name, and Fitzgerald is such a common name anyway. I wasn't careful enough at the start. My face went viral for a couple of months. And if they find me again, a picture of me will fetch a very large sum."

"If they find you."

"I'm sure it's a strong possibility. One day, some low-life will get lucky and change my life forever."

"I hope that won't happen for a long time," Flora said and took a bunch of keys from her handbag. "Let's go into the house and you can have a good look around." She started to walk toward the house.

He followed her. "Yes. I want to see that locked room."

"I have the key to it here," Flora said.

Ross waggled his eyebrows. "Let's go and unlock the secret chamber."

But the room was empty. Ross looked around. "Weird. There's a feeling here…"

"Of what?" Flora asked. She sniffed the air. "There's a strange smell."

"Paint," Ross said and pointed at the floor. "Look. Paint stains. Oil paint, I think. Of the kind you use when painting a picture on a canvas."

"Someone must have used this room as a studio."

"Quite recently too," Ross remarked. He walked to the bay window. "Gorgeous view of Nice from here. It must get the morning sun. I think I might make this my bedroom."

"Slow down," Flora laughed. "You haven't bought the house yet."

He turned and looked at her with fire in his eyes.

"Let's do it then. Flora, help me buy this house."

Chapter 11

When Flora returned to the office, there was an email from Chantal.

Flora, please find attached a brief summary of the process of selling a house in France.

Flora opened the attachment and took a quick look at the document to get the most important points. The process of selling a house in France didn't look too complicated. First, you had to make the buyer sign a 'bon de visite':

This confirms to the vendor that the agent is the one who showed them a particular house. It prevents conflicts between agents. The price of the property displayed in any advertisement includes the agent's fees, which in the case of Agence du Soleil, is ten percent. This does not include the fee for the notaire (the actual contract process will be handled by a notaire as they are the only persons permitted by law to perform conveyancing in France).Make sure you tell the buyer this usually costs between two and eight percent of the net price of a house. The notaire is required by law to act impartially and acts for both buyer and seller.

This seemed strange to Flora, but if that was the case, who was she to argue? The ten-percent fee seemed steep but probably lucrative, especially with expensive villas like the one Ross was buying. No wonder Chantal was so anxious to close the deal.

Flora skimmed through the rest of the document, noting

there were two contracts for the buyer, first the *compromise de vente*, with a ten-percent down payment on the house, then the *acte authentique* which was the final contract. There were some bits about clauses and conditions, which she would study later. But the most pressing thing at that moment was to tell Chantal the good news about Ross buying the house. She picked up the phone.

"Chantal?" Flora said when she heard the familiar voice. "Good news. Ross is buying the house. Full asking price. I'll ask him to sign the—" She glanced at the computer screen. "*Compromise de vente* and deposit ten percent of the price into our account today."

There was silence at Chantal's end.

"Chantal? Are you there? Did I call you at a bad moment? Maybe you can call me back later and tell me how to contact the vendor."

"No," Chantal said in a voice full of tears. "No need."

"Why? What—?" What was going on? Why wasn't Chantal happy about the sale? Maybe her husband was worse? "I'm sorry. Should have texted you first," Flora said, mentally kicking herself for her haste in calling Chantal.

"It's all right. I needed to know. You see, the sellers…"

"Yes? The sellers?"

"Well, they're friends of mine. They asked me to act for them. They've given me power of attorney. So I'll sign the contracts for them."

"I see. I'll get in touch later with the details."

"Yes. Let me know when he's paid the deposit."

* * *

Ross paid the deposit the next day, and the sale went through very quickly after that. Flora didn't hear from him again, but she walked past the house two weeks later when she was on a long Sunday walk with Daisy to the tip of the Cap. The house was hidden by scaffolding, and she noticed that a high wall was being built around the garden, including a tall wrought-iron gate.

"Look," Daisy said. "The new owner is doing up that house. Putting on a new roof and building a high wall all around it. And that gate will probably have an intercom and a CCT camera. Who did you say had bought it?"

"I didn't."

"But you handled the sale. You must know."

"The new owner's Canadian."

"Man or woman?"

"Man."

Daisy shoved Flora with her elbow. "Come on, spill. I can tell there's a lot more to it than that."

Flora opened her mouth to reply, trying to think of something bland and plausible but was interrupted by someone calling her name. She turned and saw Ross, dressed in his usual T-shirt and shorts sitting in a battered jeep that had just pulled up behind them. He beamed at her.

"Hi! Nice to see you. Sorry, I've been meaning to call you but I've been so busy."

"I can see that," Flora said. "You've started on the house already."

"Couldn't wait." Ross laughed and jumped out of the jeep to join them. "I want to move in as soon as possible."

Daisy looked from Flora to Ross. "So you're the new owner." She held out her hand. "I'm Daisy. From New York. You must be…?"

Ross grabbed her hand and shook it. "Ross Fitzgerald. Happy to meet you, Daisy."

"Yeah, me too," Daisy chortled. "So how are things in Toronto?"

He laughed. "Montreal. But you have a good ear for accents. What are you doing so far away from home?"

"I could ask the same thing," Daisy retorted. "But let's not get personal so soon."

"No, better not," Ross agreed. "Not that I wouldn't mind that at all." He winked at Daisy, who blushed. "Hey," he continued. "If you've nothing better to do, you might like to see how the house is progressing? Flora will want to make sure I'm not breaking any laws, in any case."

Daisy glanced at Flora. "What's he talking about?"

"It's the new face of the agency she works for," Ross replied. "Honesty and accountability. Abiding by the law."

Daisy's jaw dropped. "What? I never heard anything about that. I work there, so I should know." She glared at Flora. "But I suppose now you're the boss you can do what you like and not share it with the lowly staff."

Flora squirmed. "I was going to talk it through with you and Iris, but we've been so busy lately. It's something I've been thinking about a lot lately. I want to develop this idea and make some changes to the website and—" She stopped and looked to Ross for help.

"Shit, I'm sorry, Flora," Ross said, looking sheepish. "I shouldn't have said anything. I didn't know Daisy worked for you."

"Neither did I," Daisy grumbled. "I thought I worked for the agency and for Chantal."

Ross shifted from one foot to the other, looking uncomfortable. "Come on, girls. It's a lovely day. And it's Sunday. It's a sin to argue on a lovely Sunday. Let's go and look at the house instead. What do you say?" He smiled pleadingly at Daisy.

Daisy sighed, looking up at him. Her expression softened. "I can never resist a cute guy who begs. And I'm dying to see the house."

"Yes, come on," Flora urged, anxious to change the hostile atmosphere. She started to walk toward the house. "Give us the grand tour of the mansion, Ross. Well talk about this later, Daisy."

"You bet we will," Daisy muttered as she followed Flora.

They went through the entrance, where the tall gates hadn't yet been installed and up the garden path, past the swimming pool, restored with blue mosaic tiling, and the flowerbeds with newly planted rosebushes. The house, covered in scaffolding, loomed above them. Flora could see that the plasterwork was being replaced and the roof was nearly finished. The new tiles and plaster made the house look fresh and new, like a beautiful woman enhanced by a touch of make-up.

"It's going to be lovely," she said. "Just like it was in the old days."

Ross nodded. "Yes. I'm trying to keep the period feel and look."

"This can't be cheap," Daisy remarked. "You seem to be doing everything at once."

"I am," Ross agreed. "Inside and out. I'm having a new kitchen installed, the bathrooms updated and the whole interior repainted. I've found a great interior designer who specialises in this kind of restoration. And the architect who's handling the exterior is also researching gardens and how they would have looked in the nineteen thirties."

"You must be loaded," Daisy said. She clapped a hand to her mouth. "Oops. That just slipped out. I didn't mean to be rude."

Ross laughed while he glanced at Flora. "That's okay. And yeah, I have money. I bought a lottery ticket six months ago in Boston. I won quite a lot of money. I nearly died of shock."

Daisy looked awestruck. "Gee, that's awesome. What did you do before you won all that money?"

"I worked in McDonald's," Ross replied. "And dreamed about winning some money."

"And then it came through," Daisy chortled.

Ross beamed. "It sure did."

"Fabulous," Daisy sighed.

They entered the house, where the smell of paint permeated the air. Flora noted that most of the walls had been painted white and the parquet floors had been restored and polished. The new kitchen looked exactly as it would have when the house was built, with oak cupboards, marble worktops and a ceramic sink. All the appliances were state of the art but looked curiously nineteen thirtyish.

"I tried to pick things that would look kind of functionalist" Ross said when he noticed Flora eyeing the stainless steel cooker and fridge. "Although they're completely modern, they have that look, don't you think?"

"Absolutely," Flora agreed, glancing out the window. "I see you're planting a herb garden. Are you into cooking, then?"

"Very much," he said. "I love cooking. I like trying out new recipes. Jamie Oliver's one of my foodie heroes."

"That's strange coming from someone who used to work in McDonald's," Daisy remarked.

"I worked there," Ross said. "That doesn't mean I actually ate the stuff."

Daisy shrugged. "Yeah, sure, why would you?"

The living room was the only room that had been finished, and they admired two low white sofas, turned towards the huge picture windows. It felt as if the sky and the intensely blue sea invaded the whole room, making it glimmer with a blue light.

"This is truly magic," Flora said. "I feel like I'm floating between the sky and the sea."

"Fantastic," Daisy said. Then she fell silent, looking at Ross as if trying to figure him out.

Upstairs, the bedrooms had a cosier feel, with wallpaper with tiny flowers, birds and bees in muted colours. The bathrooms had been completely restored and cracked basins and bathtubs replaced by pieces found in architectural salvage yards.

"Just like something from The Great Gatsby." Daisy sighed and perched on a roll-top bath facing a window overlooking the sea. "Imagine lying in your bath and looking at that view."

"I'm looking forward to that," Ross said. "It'll be something I'd do more in the wintertime, though."

Flora pointed at the small fireplace. "You can have a fire in here, too. Incredible how they thought of everything when they built this house."

Ross nodded. "Yes. I'm going to do some research to find out who had this house built. I'd love to know something about the people who lived here first."

"Good idea," Flora agreed. "I love knowing the history of an old house."

"You know the poster of the mosaic downstairs?" Ross asked. "I think it's something to do with a young girl who used to live here in the sixties. One of my new neighbours mentioned her and said she was a beautiful child. I'd love to find out more about her and where she is now."

"Yes," Flora said. "So would I. She looks like someone but I can't figure out who."

"What poster?" Daisy asked. "I didn't notice a poster when we came in."

"In the hall," Ross replied. "But I took it down when they were painting. It's a framed poster of an old Greek mosaic from Delos. But the neighbour said the father of the young girl got it in Greece and had it framed because it looked so like his daughter."

Daisy looked suddenly interested. "I'd love to see it."

"I put it in the cloakroom," Ross said. "Let's go downstairs. Not much more to see here anyway."

When Ross produced the picture from the cloakroom, Daisy peered at it. "Reminds me of someone, too. Maybe it's an actress? Or a TV personality? Those eyes, so bright and expressive, even in a mosaic. Beautifully done."

Ross leaned the picture against the wall. "Even better in real life. It's a mosaic on a floor in one of those ruined houses on Delos. I saw them when I was twelve. I couldn't stop looking at them. The colours were still so vivid."

"Must be amazing," Flora said. "But we'd better get going or we'll never finish that walk."

"Yes," Daisy agreed. "We're doing the cliff walk around the Cap. And then I have a date tonight, so I want to get ready."

Ross looked at his watch. "And I have to go down to the marina to see about a mooring for my boat. I'm hoping to fix that up before I go windsurfing later. The wind's shifting to the east, which is great."

Daisy looked at him with admiration. "You windsurf? I'd love to come and watch. My boyfriend's a windsurfer, too. Maybe you'd like to meet him and his gang? They all meet for a beer at the bar at the town end of the Salis beach around seven o'clock."

Ross smiled. "I'd love that. I'll pop in sometime during the evening."

"Great," Daisy said. "See you then." She looked at Flora. "Let's get going then. It's a long walk but we have a lot to talk about."

"I suppose," Flora said, not looking forward to the next half hour. Daisy had that steely look in her eyes that meant trouble.

But Daisy didn't talk about Flora's plans for the agency as they walked down the hill. She looked over her shoulder at Ross who was getting into his jeep. "Nice guy. But he's one big liar. He didn't come into money suddenly."

Flora stared at her, mystified. "How do you mean? How else did he get it?"

"He was born with it."

* * *

Chantal went to the cafeteria to get a cup of coffee while the doctors examined Jean. He had woken up and was more lucid when he spoke to her. His left arm and leg were weak, and although his speech was slurred, he could swallow, which was a very good sign, the nurse said.

Chantal sat down at a table beside the window and stirred her coffee absentmindedly while looking out at the front steps of the hospital, wishing she could be somewhere else on such a hot sunny day. How lovely it would be to lie on a beach somewhere and feel the heat of the sun. What was Gabriel doing on such a day? He was probably with his parents and brothers at the family house in St Tropez, swimming in the pool and then drying off lying on a chaise longue. Or up in the hills with his easel painting yet another wonderful landscape. Her mind drifted to those early days when they were so in love, so passionate and hot for each other.

She resisted him for a long time. If their relationship became intimate, she would have had to compromise her moral standards and her feelings for Jean. Gabriel insisted, told her, she didn't need to feel guilty. Jean was only her husband in name. The person he had been was gone. Although Chantal agreed with him, she was consumed by guilt.

With his talent being recognised and applauded in the media, Gabriel was becoming famous and often appeared on television in cultural programmes and discussions. Women followed him around because of his charm and good looks, and he was invited to glamorous parties. He was the darling of the Riviera, which both annoyed and amused him. His rise to fame and Chantal's fear of discovery forced them to meet in secret.

It happened by accident. Chantal joined Gabriel for lunch at a little restaurant in St Tropez, little known and out of the way. It was late September and despite the glorious sunshine the air was cool and crisp. She left Jean playing *boules* in the square around the corner from their apartment. He would shuffle home later that afternoon, and their neighbour would keep an eye on him until Chantal went home.

They sat under the acacia trees and enjoyed a lunch of quiche, fresh figs and some very ripe camembert, sharing a carafe of rather rough wine.

"Not exactly a *grand cru*," Gabriel said as he sipped the wine. "But it goes well with the cheese, don't you think?"

"Absolutely," she said looking into his luminous grey eyes.

He smiled. "You're not listening."

"I'm listening to what you're not saying. And it's making me blush."

"You have good ears." He lifted up a strand of her hair. "Lovely ears." He kissed her neck just below her earlobe. "Come with me to my house," he whispered. "There's nobody there today. I want to show you where I spent my childhood summers."

She knew what he meant and what would happen if she went with him. She looked at him without replying, her stomach in a knot. She suddenly couldn't eat. She bit her lip, hesitating.

His expression was serious as their eyes met. "Chantal. Come with me. If you don't, we can't go on seeing each other. We can't stay in limbo like this. Either we say goodbye now or jump into the dark void of being—" He stopped.

"Lovers?" she whispered.

He took her hand and caressed the palm and then bent his dark head and kissed it. "Yes," he said, holding her hand against his cheek.

"The dark void?" she said, confused.

"Either choice will be difficult and painful. But being lovers will be more risky, of course."

"And wonderful," she whispered. Knowing she was taking a step into something she would regret, she nevertheless rose and held out her hand. "Come, then, my lovely Gabriel, my angel. Let's take that risk and jump into the unknown. We only live once and life is so short. I want to be happy again and feel beautiful and young. It might be my last chance."

He jumped up, paid the bill and swept her out of the restaurant, taking her hand and running up the hill so fast, she could hardly keep up in her tight skirt and high heels. She was about to beg him to slow down, when he came to a stop in front of a set of gates. He punched a number into the pad and the gates slid open. He grabbed her hand again and pulled her through the gates that immediately closed behind them with a loud bang. They walked up a gravel path lined with oleander bushes still in bloom, to an old house covered in ivy.

"Beautiful house," Chantal panted.

"Yes. Old and beautiful and big and welcoming. Usually full of people but today everyone is away, even the maid."

"Everyone?"

"My big, crazy, happy family—my parents, my brothers, their wives and children. This house has ten bedrooms, plenty of space for everyone. Do you want to see mine?"

"Your what?"

"My bedroom, *chérie*." He grabbed her hand again and pulled her through the front door. "It's upstairs."

His excitement was contagious, and Chantal felt a surge of joy as they ran up the beautiful curved staircase, across a landing, down a corridor and into a large bedroom with windows overlooking an overgrown garden and a swimming pool.

She didn't get a chance to look around. Gabriel slammed the door shut behind them and immediately took her in his arms. His urgency ignited a flame that grew to a fire impossible to quench. She ripped his shirt open while he slid her skirt down her hips. Kissing her breasts, he gently unbuttoned her silk blouse while she unzipped his trousers. Wriggling out of the rest of their clothes, they sank down on the bed naked, kissing, licking, touching.

"Slow down," Gabriel whispered and pulled back for a moment, looking at Chantal, his eyes caressing her body. "Mon amour. You are so lovely, so perfect."

She let her eyes feast on his toned body, his long limbs and golden skin. "And you, my Adonis, my angel."

"Not so angelic now." He kissed her again, his tongue probing deep into her mouth, his hands sliding over her breasts, down to her stomach, her hips and her buttocks, cupping them and pulling her so close against him she could feel he was as ready as she was. She took a deep breath. This was it. The moment when she fell into the abyss of adultery, from which there would be no going back. But she wanted it so much, wanted *him* so much. She sighed and let it happen. The moment of fear passed, and she gave herself up to the sheer joy of making love with a man who truly desired her.

When the fire abated, they lay still, looking at each other with wonder. She touched his face. He smiled. There was no need for words. It would have been impossible to voice their feelings or analyse what had happened. They both knew that saying anything would ruin the magic and shatter the mood. They simply lay there in each other's arms while the golden sunlight caressed their bodies and the cooing of doves made better music than any symphony.

He stretched and sighed. She rolled over on her side and slowly got up, padding across the cool floor tiles to the bathroom she had glimpsed through an open door. She looked over her shoulder. "I'll just have a shower before I leave."

"I wish you didn't have to go. I wish we could spend the rest of the day together."

She sighed. "Me too. But I have to leave this dream world and get back to my duties."

"I—" He stiffened as a voice from downstairs broke the silence. "Merde. My sister-in-law and her kids. What are they doing here? They're supposed to be in Nice."

Chantal panicked. "What am I going to do?" she hissed, frozen to the spot.

"Have your shower. Then we can sneak out through the back door and down the lane through the side entrance. Don't worry. Nobody will see you."

Chantal nodded and ran to the bathroom and had a quick wash. Then they both threw on their clothes and when they were ready, tiptoed through the corridor, down the narrow back stairs and out into the back lane. Chantal's secret life had begun.

Chapter 12

"What do you mean, born with it?" Flora panted, trying to keep up with Daisy, who was half-running down the hill towards the shoreline and the start of the coast walk. "Born into what?"

"Money." Daisy stopped in front of the steps leading down to the path that wound itself around the shoreline of Cap d'Antibes. "That guy isn't some pauper who worked in McDonald's and suddenly won a huge fortune. He was born rich. I can tell."

Flora stared at her. "How?"

"Well, for a start, did you notice his watch? An old Patek Philippe watch. That's usually passed from father to son."

"So? He could have bought it somewhere."

"Where? Those watches are hardly ever sold. That's a Patek Calatrava from the nineteen fifties, so he must have got it from someone. I bet you'll find the initials engraved on the back of it."

"How do you know so much about it?" Flora enquired.

"I once dated a guy who worked for Christie's. He specialised in vintage watches. He told me a lot about it. You'd be surprised how much an old watch like that would fetch. I'd say that one would be around twenty thousand dollars."

"But, as I said, he could have bought it," Flora argued. "He can certainly afford it."

"A guy suddenly coming into millions would be more

likely to buy a new Rolex or something. Then the way he's dressed," Daisy breezed on. "When it comes to shoes, anyway. Docksiders that are scuffed and torn. And that jeep—an old Range Rover."

"So?" Flora shrugged. "He could be into vintage, big time."

"Nah, I don't buy that. People who suddenly get a lot of money buy everything brand new. And then the way he's so knowledgeable about architectural history and how to restore an old house. He saw the mosaics in Delos when he was twelve, he said. How did he get there? On a cheap flight? Not very likely. And the way he speaks. Very educated and well brought up. That guy screams old money."

Flora thought for a moment. What Daisy said rang true somehow. Ross was very confident and sure of what he wanted to do. He didn't behave like someone of limited means who had suddenly become rich. It wasn't the fact that he wanted to hide, which was normal enough, it was his whole demeanour that didn't quite fit with his story.

"But what does it matter?" she said, as if to herself. "If he *is* some famous, rich heir, he obviously doesn't want anyone to find out. If he's on the run from the media, he's creating a smokescreen or something. Are we going to spy on him until we find out what's really going on? I like him and he obviously wants to make friends. What's wrong with that?"

"Nothing, I suppose," Daisy said and started to walk again. "I like him, too. He's very cute and very nice. Like a big puppy. Not like that sexy guy who took you out to dinner. What happened to him, by the way? Did you have a row? You never said anything about him."

"He turned out to be a real creep," Flora said with a dart of regret. She hadn't been able to forget Philippe and their evening. The discovery that he had used her caused her a lot of pain. She felt a sense of shame about having had sex with him so readily and decided not to tell Daisy. She would never see him again, anyway. "I don't want to talk about it if you don't mind," she said.

"That's okay. I understand," Daisy replied. "Come on. Let's do the walk, and then you can tell me what the hell you've been up to behind my back at the agency."

They walked on, Daisy taking the lead. As they rounded the corner, Flora was bowled over by the spectacular views of the sea and the coastline. The path was rough, with steps hewn out of the rocks with vertiginous drops and hair-raising climbs. Wild flowers grew in sheltered coves and the foliage of bushes and trees gave off a pungent smell of pine mixed with sage and wild rosemary.

Flora felt the muscles in her legs strain and her heart pound as she followed Daisy, who was walking swiftly ahead without looking back. She had obviously changed her mind about that talk. It gave Flora a chance to plan what she was going to say and how she would explain her ideas to Daisy. It might have been a good thing that Ross had mentioned it, as Flora had put her plans on hold while they were finalising existing sales. The English couple had offered a reduced price for the old ruined house near la Tourette sur Loup, and the owners were considering it. Flora had high hopes they would accept the offer. That house had been for sale for three years. It would be a relief to the owners to finally sell it, even at a reduced price.

As she rounded a boulder, Flora saw Daisy sitting on a flat rock, looking out at sea, the wind whipping her hair around her face. She turned as Flora approached.

"Let's take a rest. We can talk here."

"Okay." Flora wiped the sweat from her brow and joined Daisy on the rock. "I'm a little tired, actually."

"Yeah. Me too. This isn't an easy walk."

"A bit hard on the legs all right."

"Sure is."

They were silent for a while, both looking out at sea and

a sailing boat far out at the blue horizon. Then Daisy turned to Flora.

"So, what was that all about, then? Honesty and accountability? A new image for the agency?"

Flora brushed her hair back from her face. "Yes, well, it was an idea. Something a client said a few weeks ago… that the agency wasn't honest and that we lured people to buy houses that aren't up to standard. That the photos on the website and in the brochures are enhanced to look like dream houses."

"Of course they are. What's wrong with that?"

"I agree. All the agencies around here do it. And initially, I didn't think it that big a deal. A fib here and there, lying by omission when you don't explain planning laws and water charges, flirting with the mayor or paying him a little bit on the side to get him to bend the rules. Not caring much when a buyer has paid for the house and is then hit with problems we can't be sued for."

Daisy turned to face her. "So what happened to change your mind?"

Flora stared out to sea and the sailing boat that was just a little white dot on the horizon. "What changed my mind? A few little things all put together—that English woman with all her dreams and wishes, needing a peaceful place to make her happy again. She fell in love with this house, but her husband said they couldn't afford it. She wouldn't have viewed it if the photo in the brochure hadn't been so alluring. Then I was supposed to lie and say that it would be easy to fix up and that they could get water and electricity connected easily, when I knew it wasn't going to be easy at all. But the husband was on to me and made me feel ashamed. So I told him the truth and that I'd try to get the sellers to lower their price. The husband then said he'd be interested if the price was lower. You should have seen the woman's face when she was told there would be a chance they'd get the house. It was as if she'd been handed hope on a plate. Hope for a better life and solace at last." Flora drew breath.

"You're too soft for this job," Daisy said dryly.

"Probably. But you know what? After that, things happened that made me feel as if this is meant to be."

"What things?"

"Well, first of all the evening with Philippe. It was wonderful, you know. Really magical. But then I found out what he really does for a living." Tears welled up as Flora remembered.

"What?" Daisy urged. "Come on, tell me. He's a pimp with a string of hookers?"

"No, of course not!"

"What then? He pushes heroin to teenagers? Sells porn on the Internet?"

"Stop it." Flora laughed despite her misery. "No, he's a paparazzo. He sneaks up on celebrities when they're not looking and takes pictures, and then he sells them all over the world for a lot of money."

"Is that all? Okay, that's bad when you think about it," Daisy agreed. "I bet he was using you as some kind of prop at that restaurant, too. Pretty sneaky."

"Yes."

"Was the sex good?"

"Yes." Flora shivered. "How did you know?"

Daisy shrugged. "Easy. You came home so late and looked so dreamy the next day. And then you freaked out about something and wouldn't tell me."

"I see. Well, anyway," Flora continued, not wanting to dwell on her heartache about Philippe. "That evening, Chantal rang me and said she wanted me to run the agency while she looks after her husband. So I thought this would be my chance to change the face of the agency and how we deal with buyers. It seemed the right thing to do, for some reason. Plus, when I thought about Philippe and what he does and how he earns all that money, I knew I didn't want to be a part of that kind of scam. Or any kind of scam, really. Fooling people, using their dreams to sell houses. Don't you see how wrong that is?"

Daisy fiddled with her hair. "Hmm, yes, I suppose. I must admit it would feel very good to be honest and try to help people. But we'd be taking a huge risk. If you start telling the truth about the properties and put up pictures showing the flaws, won't we lose clients instead of gaining more? The sellers would go to other agencies. Chantal will be livid when she finds out. That's the scariest part."

Flora nodded. "I know. But I have a feeling Chantal isn't really focusing on the agency right now. I just tell her everything is fine when she calls and she says 'good' and hangs up. Not like her at all. So we have a bit of a window here, you know. And if it looks like it's not working, we can always turn it around again and go back to what we were."

"But you're taking advantage of Chantal's husband's illness to do something behind her back. Isn't that a little scammy in itself?" Daisy asked.

Flora nodded. "Yes. It is. But it's all for a very good cause. When Chantal returns in a couple of months, she'll see a whole new agency with happy clients and a squeaky clean reputation."

"And loads and loads of pigs flying around." Daisy snorted. "I don't think much of your idea. I mean, it's all very noble, of course. But wouldn't it be better to be more subtle?"

Flora frowned. "How do you mean?"

"If we don't change the photos in the brochures or anything on the website, it will all look perfectly normal to the sellers. But when we do talk to buyers, we could tell them the truth about properties that are a bit dicey. We could also stop lying about planning permission and water charges and all that stuff. We could concentrate on the properties that have been for sale for a long time and tell those sellers to lower their prices. Negotiate a bit. Try to meet everyone halfway. That way everyone will be happy and Chantal needn't know a thing. It could even result in some of those old shacks finally being sold. And the agency will slowly gain a good reputation without shouting about it or taking risks."

Flora stared at Daisy in awe. "You're a fecking genius."

Daisy beamed, taking on a look of fake modesty. "I know."

"What will Iris think?"

"She'll spit nails but what do we care? We can take it, right?"

"Of course," Flora said without conviction. Iris would be difficult to convince.

Daisy jumped up from the rock. "Let's get going. I suddenly feel full of beans. I'm really looking forward to getting back to work now." She turned and started jogging up the steps to where the path was bordered by a high wall bristling with security cameras and lights.

"Who lives behind those walls?" Flora panted as she tried to keep up with Daisy.

"Russians," Daisy shouted, pulling ahead. "Russian oligarchs who have bought up half the coast and slapped up these ugly walls. Don't you just hate them?"

"Horrible," Flora agreed. "I hope we never have to deal with them."

"Nah, our agency is small potatoes to the big shots."

They rounded a bend and arrived at a gateway and a road leading up the hill to the bus stop.

Daisy stopped and bent over, putting her hands on her knees, breathing hard. "Phew. That was a tough sprint."

Flora wiped the sweat off her face with the sleeve of her T-shirt. "Yeah. I'm not as fit as I thought."

As they walked up the road, they had to step aside as a motorbike roared down towards them. Flora waited for it to pass, but it stopped and the motorcyclist took off his helmet and peered at her. "Flora?"

"Philippe. What are you doing here?

Philippe smiled. "I'm on a job. Don't worry, it's a fashion shoot. Perfectly respectable."

"I see."

Daisy looked from Flora to Philippe. "Hey, I have to go. I'll leave you guys to talk." Without waiting for a reply, she walked swiftly up the hill without glancing back.

They looked at each other. Flora knew she should walk away but she couldn't. She stepped away until her back was against the hot wall. Her eyes drank in his handsome face, velvet eyes and strong hands gripping the handlebars of the bike. The hands that had caressed her when they made love. Sweat broke out on her face, and she tried to wipe it away with the back of her hand.

"I have to go," she said and sidled away.

He put his hand on her arm. "I'm sorry. I behaved badly. Shouldn't have used you like that."

"Okay. Apology accepted."

"Thank you." He fiddled with the strap of his helmet. "So how are you? The agency business going well?"

"Very well."

He seemed to hesitate. "That's good. I saw you sold that house up on the hill—Les Temps Heureux."

"That's right."

"Must have gone for a couple of million."

She nodded, knowing what he would ask next. "Something like that."

"Whoever bought it is building a high wall. I saw when I drove past. It must be someone who needs a lot of privacy. I suppose you're not going to tell me who it is?"

Flora bristled. "Right again."

His eyes turned cold. "I understand." Without another word, he kickstarted the bike and roared down the hill at breakneck speed.

* * *

The second time they made love, Chantal started to cry.

"What's wrong?" Gabriel asked her. "Did I hurt you?"

"No." Chantal hid her face in the folds of the sheet. "It's just the thought I had. Of how I'm cheating on Jean."

Gabriel pulled the sheet from her face. "Look at me, Chantal. You are not cheating on Jean. He's not the man he was. If he was in good health, yes, that would be cheating. But he's not. His whole personality has changed, you said. He's like a child. You have to look after him like an invalid. That's not a marriage."

"But I said 'till death do us part,'" Chantal sobbed. "'For better or worse.'"

"I know. You did."

"God will punish me for this. I'll go to hell."

"I don't believe in hell." Gabriel rolled onto his back and put his hands under his head. "I think hell is right here, in this world, not the next." He turned to her again. "Chantal, my darling, you're a beautiful, sensual woman. How could any god, if there is such a thing, want you to suffer? Isn't it enough that you look after Jean and make sure he has everything he needs? Isn't he, in his present state, quite happy?"

Chantal nodded and wiped her face with the sheet. "He's like a little boy. And yes, quite happy. But it breaks my heart to watch this intelligent, kind, attractive mind sink into a state of simply existing. Of just eating, sleeping, playing boules with the old men and then watching silly TV programmes in the evening until he falls asleep and I have to wake him and help him into bed." She turned and looked at Gabriel, her eyes caressing his handsome face, his thick brown hair and beautiful grey eyes. "I had no life until I met you. It was all work, shopping, cooking and looking after Jean. We used to have such a lively social life and such a wide circle of friends. We travelled, went to the theatre and concerts. And then in a very short time it all ended. I had to take over the agency and that wasn't easy. Still isn't."

He touched her face. "It's so sad for you both. I know you still love him. How could you not?"

She caught his hand. "I do. But I love you too, Gabriel. You saved my life, in a way, and my sanity."

"And you mine. Don't misunderstand me when I say this. But I love our secret life and that nobody knows about us." He looked around the room of the empty house where they met whenever they could escape from their normal lives. "And this house, this room is like a haven away from eyes and ears and nasty gossip. I'm so glad we can meet here, high up in the hills and love each other for short moments. I'm only sorry we have to hide like this, but my life has become so complicated since that exhibition only a few months ago."

She smiled. "You're famous now. Fame can be hard to cope with. But I'm glad your wonderful work gets the attention and the praise it deserves."

"Thank you." He rose from the bed and pulled on a dressing gown he kept there, along with towels and toiletries they had both taken to this empty house, her house, that would soon be put up for sale. It had been Chantal's idea to meet there, and she had arranged to have some furniture delivered: a bed, two easy chairs and a small table, which they put in front of the picture windows overlooking the Bay of Angels. One furnished bedroom in a big, empty house: their secret hideaway.

"La Baie des Anges," he said, standing by the window. "A beautiful name for a beautiful stretch of water."

She pulled the sheet around her and joined him at the window. "I love the story of how it got its name. You know, how Adam and Eve were standing outside the gates of the Garden of Eden, having been locked out because they ate the forbidden fruit. And then they heard a rustle of wings and discovered an angel who guided them to this spot. Nearly as beautiful as the Garden of Eden, and they settled there for the rest of their lives."

"Or," he said, still gazing at the view, "the story of the young Christian girl who was persecuted by the Romans, beheaded and put in a boat that was set adrift across the sea. The angels guided the boat into the same bay where they had guided Adam and Eve all those years before. The bones of Sainte Réparate are in the cathedral in the Old Town which bears her name, in Place Rossetti."

"Well, that story's difficult to believe," Chantal remarked. "The date on her grave says she died in ten sixty. Are you saying her boat was adrift for eight hundred years?"

He laughed. "The most plausible story is that the bay got its name from the angel sharks that have fins like wings. So the fishermen called this bay after them."

"I prefer the Adam and Eve story," Chantal said. "And the angel might have been your namesake. But the fish story is probably the true one. It doesn't take away the beauty, whatever the legends say."

He turned back to the view. "I never tire of looking at it. And it's never the same. Look how the buildings are given a pink glow from the late afternoon sun and the contrast of the intense blue of the water. This late in October, the light is so mellow and melancholy. I'd like to paint it just like this."

"It's stunning today. But the light reminds me I have to go. I only had this hour to myself today. I have to do the shopping on the way home and pick Jean up from the harbour where he's wandering around, looking at the boats. Sometimes he can't remember the way home, even though it's only a few minutes' walk away." She put her hand on his shoulder. "You should bring your easel here. You could paint that view. The light is lovely at this time of year."

He kept looking at the view, his hand on hers. "I'd like to paint this view at different times of day and do something like a triptych. Or a Monet kind of thing."

"You mean like he did with the cathedral of Rouen but in a landscape? I like that idea."

He turned and looked at her. "I'd like to paint you. Not all of you but elements of you. They could be part of those paintings. This view and then you in the corner, looking out of the window, turning your head and your eyes reflecting the blue of the bay. Your hair blowing in the wind…bits of you, your spirit, your *being*, in every one of those paintings."

She sighed, her hand falling from his shoulder. "I will be in them, even if you don't paint me."

He nodded, shivering in the chill of the draught from the open window. "Of course you will."

"And now I have to go." She got dressed, tidied the bed and walked to the door. "*A bientôt, mon amour.*" She kissed her fingers, pressed them on his cheek and left, softly closing the door behind her. She crept down the creaking stairs and slipped through the silent front garden and opened the old gate, peering into the deserted street. Nobody there. She quickly got into her car and drove away, her mind full of Gabriel and the afternoon they had spent together. This secret life. This hidden love affair. So hard but at the same time exhilarating.

Sitting by Jean's bed, she remembered how she carried the memories of her tryst with Gabriel around with her everywhere, giving her sudden darts of pleasure and joy all through her dreary existence. It was her delicious secret, like wearing sexy lingerie under everyday clothes. And despite her feelings of guilt, she had do admit to herself that the secrecy was a big part of the excitement. She didn't want it to end.

* * *

Iris didn't react positively to the agency's change of policy.

"What?" she screeched. "We're going to be *honest*? What the hell do you mean? How are we going to sell *anything* if we tell buyers the fucking truth? I've spent *hours* on the phone just now, lying through my teeth to a German so he'd be lured—I mean convinced—to view a property that's just come up for sale. It's one of those so-called villas in that god-awful holiday complex, but it's near a good beach and has great views. The house itself is crap, but I'm going over there later today to get it tarted up a bit and to make sure the pool's cleaned so it doesn't have that awful smell. But now you tell me we have to show it warts and all?" Iris looked incredulously at Flora. "I'm going to tell this man it's a badly built house that will be boiling in the summer and freezing in the winter? That the plumbing is so bad the toilet backs up into the bath if he flushes it too often and that there's a huge problem with mosquitoes because of that pond the *commune* refuses to drain?" She drew breath and glanced at Daisy, pointing at her head and rolling her eyes.

Flora, standing in front of Iris in the outside office, folded her arms. "Yes. That's it in a nutshell. Well, with some adjustments, but yeah, the truth is king from now on."

Iris turned to Daisy, who was looking at her computer screen with great concentration. "Daisy? What are you saying? Do you agree with this?"

Daisy looked up. "Uh, yes."

"I don't believe it! How can you, Daisy?" Iris demanded. "When we've been drilled for years in Chantal's school of putting up a glossy façade. We're good at it, too. We've sold properties faster than any agency around here, and now you want to lose all of that just so Goody-Two-Shoes here can feel good about herself?"

Flora went to the door, locked it and put up the Closed/ Fermé sign. No need to have clients witnessing this tirade. She turned to Iris.

"It's not about me feeling good about myself. It's about showing buyers exactly what they're buying. In the long run, it'll work better than the earlier approach of hiding problems that come to light after the sale. How many angry buyers have you had to deal with in the past?"

"A couple," Iris mumbled.

"A week, you mean," Daisy cut in. She turned to Flora. "Chantal usually deals with angry buyers, and she's good at getting out of trouble, daring them to sue and pointing out how much lawyers cost and how difficult it is to prove it was either our or the sellers' fault that problems weren't revealed before a sale. Or that damage to property didn't happen until after a sale. They usually back off after a shouting match."

"I can't imagine Chantal shouting," Flora said. "She's usually so cool."

Daisy laughed. "She doesn't shout. She just studies her nails while she waits for them to run out of breath. Then she sighs and says something about it being a pity lawyers are so expensive and court cases take so many years before they're resolved. She's brilliant at taking the wind out of their sails."

"It's quite fun to watch," Iris remarked with a little smile.

"Yes," Daisy said. "But I've often felt really sorry for some of the disgruntled buyers. Some of those people are old and have spent their life savings on these dream houses that turn out to be more of a nightmare. That's why I was kind of happy to hear Flora's plan."

"You're taking advantage of the fact that Chantal's husband is very ill," Iris argued. "And that she'll probably be gone for months. She appointed you manager because she trusts you, Flora. And now you're abusing that trust to change everything here."

Flora sighed. "I know what you're saying, Iris. And I would have agreed with you if I was going ahead with my first plan to make this public and change the way we run things here. But then Daisy came up with the idea that instead of shouting it to the world, we should adopt a softly-softly approach and change things by stealth instead. You'll see. In the end everyone will be happy."

"Everyone except Chantal," Iris muttered and returned to her computer.

Chapter 13

The weeks flew by with astonishing speed while Flora struggled to maintain order at the agency. Daisy often sneaked off as the glorious weather and good winds made windsurfing more enticing than working in a small office. Iris reluctantly handled clients with more honesty and courtesy, and Flora tried to convince sellers to lower their prices to get a quicker sale. It was all very hit and miss at the beginning, as sellers withdrew their properties and buyers were disappointed with the more realistic picture of their dream house. But she was delighted to see some of the houses that had been on their books for years finally sporting a 'Sold' sign, albeit for a much lower price. She was able to tell Chantal sales were good and old properties finally off their books. Chantal sighed a thank you.

"How's your husband?" Flora asked.

"Better. He's recovering well. But he's being transferred to a hospital in Paris for brain surgery when he's strong enough."

"Oh, that sounds serious."

"Serious, yes. But there is a good chance he will recover fully even though rehabilitation will take a long time."

"That sounds like good news," Flora said. "Even though it will be hard at first."

"Yes. Very hard. I hope you won't mind continuing to run the agency for a while longer?"

"Absolutely not," Flora said, her shoulders relaxing. What a relief. They still had time to turn things around. "Things are going well. We've sold that house by the vineyard down the hill from Ramatuelle. Not the asking price but—"

"That old wreck? Excellent," Chantal cut in, saving Flora from having to confess the house had gone for a song. "I haven't had time to check the bank statements, but I trust you to make sure we get sales and our commissions."

"Of course."

"Good. Well, I'll say goodbye for a while," Chantal said, sounding tired. "I'll call back from Paris in a week or two. Thank you for looking after the agency so well."

"You're welcome," Flora said and hung up with just a tiny pang of guilt.

* * *

Ross called one afternoon in late June. "Hey, how are you? I haven't been in touch for a while."

"We've been very busy. And Daisy keeps bunking off to windsurf, so Iris and I are run off our feet trying to keep up."

He laughed. "My fault, I'm afraid. I've been sending her a text every time the wind's good. And then she got this new board."

"That must have cost a—" Flora stopped. "You bought it for her?"

"Uh, yes. Why not? She's such a sweetie and has introduced me to all her friends."

"Well, that's very nice," Flora snapped. "And here am I, busting my gut to run this agency practically single-handed while Daisy waltzes around keeping you amused."

"Sorry," Ross said, sounding nothing of the kind. "But, hey, why don't you take a break and come up to my house later on? We can crack open a beer or two, share a pizza or something?"

Flora calmed down. There was something beguiling about Ross that made it impossible to be cross with him for more than two seconds. "Why not? I could do with a break from all of this."

"Great. See you at around seven o'clock, then," Ross said and hung up.

Flora busied herself with the chores of doing the accounts and drawing up a schedule for the following day. There were some good houses on their books just then that wouldn't be too hard to sell. And she had a couple of enthusiastic buyers wanting to look at them. Iris would be able to handle that. Then she was meeting someone who wanted her to look over a possible property they might handle and an appointment at the mayor's office about two properties she knew would need work. She wanted to enquire ahead of time so that she was armed with as much information as possible. The days of telling buyers only what they wanted to hear were over.

By the time Flora left the office, it was six o'clock. Too early to arrive at Ross's house but just the right time to sit in a café, relax and read the evening paper with a cool drink. Bliss after a long day of talking to people.

Flora walked the short distance down the pedestrian street to the little square and found a table in the shade of a large umbrella. She ordered a glass of *citron glacé* and opened a copy of *The Daily Telegraph* she had picked up at a newsstand. It was great to catch up with news outside France for a change. She scanned the first page and only skimmed through an article about the aftermath of the Scottish elections and then moved to news of the situation in the Middle East and turned the page. World news was the same, and she had already read Nice Matin at breakfast that morning.

On the next page, a headline caught her attention: *Heir to the Herbert-Rothschild fortune spotted on the French Riviera.* Herbert-Rothschild? Who were they? Some American branch of the famous French banking family? There was a fuzzy photo of a tall dark woman standing on the deck of a yacht, holding a boy of around twelve by the hand with the caption: *The late Marie-Louise Rothschild with her son, on holiday in Greece about twenty years ago. Joseph Herbert, of the pharmaceutical millions, who was briefly married to Marie-Louise Rothschild of the French banking family, died two years ago, leaving his entire fortune to his only child, Joseph Charles Herbert Jr. This, on top of the Rothschild fortune inherited from his late mother, makes Joseph Jr a very rich young man indeed. He has not been seen since the death of his father and was believed to be hiding in the family compound in the Bahamas. As he has escaped the press for a number of years, nobody really knows what he looks like. But a former employee of the Herbert family recently reported she had seen him coming out of a club in Cannes after a night out with friends.*

Flora took a sip of her drink. How sad—all that money but having to hide from the public and the press. Money didn't buy happiness, after all.

Lost in thought, Flora didn't notice a shadow falling over her table. But then she felt the presence of someone and looked up. Philippe. Standing there looking at her in silence. She met his gaze.

"Philippe. What are you doing here?"

"Looking at you." He pulled up a chair and sat down without asking for permission.

She looked back at him, fighting to stay calm. Why did she feel so incredibly drawn to him? It wasn't the memory of that hot night; it was something else, something she couldn't control. He was bad news and would break her heart if she ever gave into him again, just like all the others. She was hurt by the way he used her and the revelation of how he earned his money turned part of her away. Her mind said no, but her heart and soul had other ideas, not to mention her libido. She crossed her legs and folded her arms over her chest to stop him looking at her breasts in the tight T-shirt. "Not much to look at."

He put his hand on her arm, caressing it with his thumb. "You're very nice to look at, Flora."

His touch sent an electric current through her. But she didn't pull her arm away. She wanted to feel his warm hand there for just a moment. She closed her eyes and enjoyed his touch for a second. Then she looked at him, knowing her eyes gave her away. "You make me feel so confused."

"In what way?"

"You know what way!" she exclaimed and pulled away from his touch.

"You do the same to me." He sighed and sat back, suddenly looking weary. "You trouble me. You occupy my thoughts every day. Every night." He shook his head. "I never felt that about a woman before."

"Yeah, I bet." Tears of frustration welled up in Flora's eyes. "I don't know if I should love you or loathe you."

"Same here. What are we going to do?"

She shrugged and wiped away the tears. "Haven't a clue."

"You hate what I do, don't you? And that I used you to get those pictures?"

She nodded, unable to speak. "Yes and yes."

"But I want to see you again. I was going to ask you out, but I didn't dare. I didn't even know if you'd speak to me." He hesitated. "Is there any way you'd agree to go out with me?"

"No," Flora replied but immediately changed her mind. "Yes. There is a way. But you might not like it."

"Tell me."

"Okay. Here's an idea. We go out on dates, but not to fancy restaurants where we might spot celebrities. And you're not allowed to bring your camera or phone. Do you think you can do that?"

He nodded, taking her hand. "I think it would be fun."

"One more condition, then."

"What's that?" he kissed her hand.

Flora looked at him sternly. "No sex."

* * *

Flora laughed to herself as she made her way up the hill to Ross's house. Philippe had looked so crestfallen when she had told him the final part of the bargain. But she liked the idea. This way they could get to know each other and not be distracted by sex. It would be nearly impossible not to fall into bed, but the fact that he had agreed to her terms told her he was serious about her. And he said he would let her decide the venues for their dates. She would call him later after she had thought of a good first 'chaste date', as she called it.

As Ross's house came into view, Flora was taken aback by the sight of the high wall surrounding the property. The security camera at the gate looked like the eye of an electronic watchdog, and it swivelled around to stare at her as she pressed the button on the intercom. A tinny voice asked her to identify herself, and giggling nervously, she spoke her name. Then there was a buzzing sound and the gate opened. Flora slipped inside and jumped as the gate slammed shut behind her. She looked around the deserted garden. Where was Ross? She hadn't seen his jeep in the street, but he probably parked it in the carport inside the wall now.

Walking up the garden path that meandered between perfectly tended flowerbeds with roses in full bloom, she turned the corner and gasped as she saw the transformation of the back of the house. The lawns had been terraced and ended in an infinity pool that hung over the steep incline of the hill, giving the impression the pool was suspended in thin air, hovering over the blue waters of the bay. It was the most beautiful swimming pool she had ever seen. She looked back at the house, shimmering in the bright sunshine, its newly painted façade pristine and the windows glinting like all-seeing eyes.

"Flora," Ross's voice called from the open French window of the ground floor. "Come here and help me with the pizza and beer. We can eat on the small terrace outside the kitchen."

Flora went to join him and helped him put the platter with the hot pizza and the bottles of beer on the table in the little courtyard outside the kitchen.

"I haven't seen you for a while. How are things?" Ross asked when they had sat down.

"Not bad. The changes at the agency are a bit complicated. But we're getting there slowly."

"And that guy you were having problems with?"

Flora grinned. "I'm working that out too."

"I can tell. You're glowing."

"That's the walk up the hill in this heat." She looked up at the façade. "You really transformed this house." She helped herself to a wedge of pizza. "And in such a short time."

He laughed and grabbed a beer. "I'm very impatient. How do you like it?"

"It's stunning, especially the pool. Wow, I couldn't stop looking at it. What have you done about the old pool at the front?"

"The new pool's great. I love swimming there after a long day of surfboarding. Especially at night, in the moonlight, when it's like floating in outer space. And the old pool will be turned into a fountain."

Flora took a slug of beer. "Where did you get the idea?"

"I saw it at a house in the Bahamas."

"The Baha—" Flora started and then suddenly knew. The hunch she had had when she read the article came back to her, and she started to put all the pieces together, all falling into place with a loud 'kerching' in her head. She choked on her beer as she connected all the dots. When she could breathe again, she wiped her mouth and stared at Ross. "You're him, aren't you?"

Startled, he stopped chewing pizza. "Him, who?"

"Joseph Herbert Junior. Sole heir to the Herbert-Roths-child fortune."

* * *

The sun slowly sank behind the Esterel Mountains in the west as Ross told Flora the story of his life. It was a sad story, and some of it made Flora's eyes well up with tears: the lonely little boy who had to witness his father's abuse of his mother until the divorce when he was left with a silent, bitter woman who spent most of her life going from one luxury hotel to the other until her untimely death of cancer five years later. His father had only contacted him once after the death of his mother, wanting to see Ross and ask for forgiveness.

"But he was drunk," Ross said. "And he cried and slob-bered all over me, saying how sorry he was and how he had regretted his behaviour ever since. But the memory of him beating up my mom is something I'll never forget or forgive. So I told him to fuck off, basically, and then I never saw him again." He shrugged, looking at his feet. "He died a couple of years ago and left me all this money. I gave a lot of it away to various charities and kept the rest."

"So how did you manage after your mother died?" Flora asked.

"I spent my teenage years in Montreal with my aunt. She organised tutors so I'd get an education without having to go to school. Then when my dad died, I moved to the Bahamas, where he had a big place. I tried to stay incognito, which isn't much fun when you're young and want to meet people your own age. There were always photographers hanging around outside our compound, trying to catch a glimpse of me and take a photo that would earn them millions. I got bored with that and bought this little yacht and proceeded to adopt a new identity. Ross Fitzgerald was my dad's uncle. I only met him once when I was a kid, but I remember him clearly. He was a great guy who loved sailing and exploring. He died up a mountain somewhere in the Rockies when he fell down a gulley and broke his neck. One of the nicest people I've ever met."

"So you named your new persona after him?" Flora asked, still recovering from the shock of her discovery.

Ross nodded. "Yes. Funny, I've used this name for about two years now. I *feel* like Ross Fitzgerald. That other guy's dead and buried. He got a rough deal in life. I don't want to be him anymore. I want to live a little and start my new life, here in this amazing place, far away from the hotspots of the world where rich people hang out. I just want to be a normal guy who happened to have come into some money, you know?"

Flora nodded, startled by the determination in the blue eyes. As he told her his story, his demeanour had changed from the happy, nearly hippy-like young man to someone who was deeply troubled by his past but determined to start afresh and make his life as good as it could get.

"I think you're very brave."

"You're not sore at me for lying?"

Flora shrugged. "Ah, sure. You didn't really lie. You *are* Ross Fitzgerald because you believe it. I never knew that other guy even existed until I read the article in The Daily Telegraph today. So, I'm just going to forget I read it. To me, you're Ross, the lucky lottery winner. Wish I could do what you did—become someone else and forget all the crap in my life."

"Why don't you? Who would you like to be? Let's make up a name and when you're down or have to face shitty people that make you feel bad about yourself, pretend you're her, that other woman who takes no prisoners."

Flora laughed. "That's a great idea. So, who should I be?"

"Let's make up a name for you. Hang on, I have an idea." He closed his eyes, looking like someone in a deep trance. "I'm getting it now. You are…" He opened his eyes and pointed at her. "Carole."

Flora blinked. "What? How many of those beers have you had?"

"Only two. But listen, it just came to me. Carole, after that nineteen forties movie star, Carole Lombard. She was married to Clark Gable, remember? Very sassy and funny. Then of course, Monroe, you know, like Marilyn Monroe. Sexy, sultry bombshell. Great combo and exactly how I see you."

"Carole Monroe." Flora laughed. "I like it. Not sure about that sexy image, but hey, who am I to complain if you see me that way?"

"And Daisy," Ross continued, not listening. "She is…she is…Venus de Milo and Grace Kelly all rolled into one."

"Venus Kelly." Flora laughed. "Gee, you have a very romantic image of her." She peered at Ross through the dim light of the gathering dusk. "Are you falling in love with our Daisy?"

Ross got up and started to collect the beer bottles on the table. "No, of course not."

"Methinks someone protests too much."

"He stopped in his stride. Okay. You're right. Daisy's very special and I'm falling for her big time. But I don't know how to tell her."

"Have you tried?"

"No. It's hopeless. She has a boyfriend and I think they're pretty hot. But let's not go there, okay?"

The pain in his voice startled Flora. He loved someone who didn't love him back. How sad. And how ironic. Thousands of women would have probably done anything to get him. But the only one *he* wanted he couldn't have.

"Of course. I don't blame you, though. Daisy is lovely."

"Yes, she is."

There was a finality in his voice that stopped Flora pursuing the subject. "Fabulous evening," she said instead, looking at the new moon rising over the umbrella pines. "But I must go. I want to get an early night. We have a lot of showings tomorrow, and I have to deal with a sale that's in danger of falling through."

He walked with her through the front garden, where the scent of the roses mingled with pine and the smell of a barbeque nearby. The bay glinted far below, and they could hear a faint scream of sirens from the main road leading to the town.

"We seem so far away from everything here," Flora remarked. "It's like a secret hideaway that nobody knows about."

"Nor will they," Ross said and pressed a button to make the gates slide silently open. "Right?"

"Not ever," Flora promised. Walking away, she heard the gates slam shut and made a firm vow to keep Ross's secret completely to herself.

Chapter 14

The 'chaste' dates proved to be very enjoyable. At least for Flora. She felt a sense of power as she decided the venue for each date and heard Philippe meekly agree to meet in McDonald's for a burger and fries, where they mingled with spotty teenagers and families with cranky toddlers. Philippe made Flora giggle when he ordered a Happy Meal for her, saying he was old enough to be her father. He wasn't, she found out, when he told her he was forty-six and showed her his French identity card to prove it. There were fourteen years between them, but she never had the feeling she was going out with an older man, as, apart from the laughter lines around his eyes and few grey hairs in his thick brown hair, he both looked and acted like someone ten years younger.

Their dates continued to delight her as they dined in pizza restaurants or bought Chinese or Thai takeaway to eat sitting on the wall of the harbour, watching the boats sailing back home in the evening sun. They went to the early morning market one Sunday and picked food for a picnic they would share later, and then Philippe took Flora on a tour of old Antibes.

Hand in hand, they strolled through the cobbled streets and alleys, looking at houses built in the Middle Ages, poking around tiny shops that sold artefacts and handmade leather goods and jewellery. Philippe bought her a necklace of multi-coloured semi-precious stones that matched her green eyes, and she bought him a leather belt. Then they visited the Picasso museum in what used to be the Château Grimaldi, built on the foundations of the ancient Greek town of Antipolis, just inside the city walls, with stunning views over the Mediterranean. Philippe lamented his lack of camera equipment as Flora stood looking out at the sea, but she reminded him of the terms to which he had agreed: no camera of any kind.

There wasn't much physical contact apart from holding hands or a light kiss on the cheek to say goodnight when Philippe took her back to her building on his motorbike. But even the light touches of his hand or his lips on her cheek made Flora tingle all over, and she would arrive at the apartment with flushed cheeks and a happy smile.

"You look like you've just got out of bed after great sex," Daisy remarked one evening, when Flora danced in through the door.

"But we're not having sex." Flora sank down on the sofa and stretched her arms over her head. "Oh, I feel so good." She let her arms drop and laughed at Daisy's puzzled face. "Yeah, okay, it's not easy for him. I can tell he's getting frustrated."

"You'll have to put him out of his misery soon or he'll screw some other woman."

"I know. And I will. When the time's right. Soon. I won't be able to stand it myself much longer, I have to admit."

"He must be crazy about you."

"Do you think so?"

Daisy nodded. "Sure, he is. Why else would he agree to this chaste stuff? He's a grown man. I bet he finds it hard to ride that bike all the way to Vence after a day of you teasing him."

"Yeah, that must be a killer." Flora giggled.

Daisy threw a pillow at her. "You cruel woman. How many more dates before you both explode?"

"Just one. Tomorrow is our sixth date and that's what we agreed. We're going to the market and then to the beach with a picnic."

"Sweet. Are you getting to know him better?"

Flora thought for a moment. "Yes. And no. We haven't talked much about our lives, but I have found out what a nice guy he really is behind that smooth façade. We have fun together and laugh at the same things. We both love art and have read the same books. Quite amazing when you consider our age difference and that we're from different countries. But he loves Ireland and has been there many times on photo trips and for holidays."

"You were made for each other," Daisy remarked with just a touch of irony in her voice. "All you need now is a great big ding-dong of a fight and then you'll know what it's like to love a Frenchman."

"I don't think we'll fight. We seem so in tune. Right now, everything's perfect."

"That's usually when fights break out."

* * *

"This is very healthy," Philippe said as he finished his sandwich. "Rye bread with tomato and chicken, one peach and a bottle of water. No wine?"

"Nope," Flora said. "Wine would make us feel all warm and fuzzy." She wiped her mouth on a tissue and tidied away the remnants of their picnic into her beach bag. She had to laugh when she saw Philippe trying to get comfortable on his beach blanket, surrounded by families and dogs on the public beach. "And we meet in public places so we're not tempted to—" She paused. "Well, you know."

"You're very cruel. In that blue swimsuit, you're both demure and sexy. I knew this was some kind of test, but I had no idea it would be like this"

"Mixing with normal people? Is that so tough?" Flora stretched out on her blanket beside Philippe and squinted at him in the bright sunlight.

"I haven't been to this beach for years."

"Welcome to the world of most people." Flora put a folded towel under her head and laughed as Philippe flinched at a dog sniffing his face. "You've been rich for too long. Time you woke up and smelled the dog poo."

"I've worked hard for what I have."

"On the backs of famous people. I mean, at the expense of them, of course," she corrected herself.

"They're crying all the way to the bank." Philippe touched her hair. "You're going blonder."

She pulled away, even that light touch making her feel hot. "It's the sun. It bleaches my hair."

"It suits you. And your skin is a lovely golden colour now."

"I am being careful, though."

"Good. Do you want me to put on some sun cream for you?"

"No. Daisy did it for me before I left. This kind lasts six hours." She nearly regretted her words. The thought of his hands smoothing cream all over her body seemed delicious—and too sexy.

"You've thought of everything." He smiled lazily, closing his eyes. "I'm just going to lie here and digest that healthy lunch and dream of what we might do together if we were somewhere more romantic."

"That's cheating."

He opened one eye. "Why is it cheating? You can't control my mind."

"I suppose." She turned over onto her stomach. "But this was supposed to be a way for us to get to know each other better. And this is our last chaste date. Unless you want to go on dating like this, of course."

"I'd rather roast in hell." He caressed her arm with the tip of his finger. "Next, we're going on my kind of date."

She wriggled away from his touch. "Last chaste date and last chance to really talk about ourselves. So don't go to sleep. Tell me about yourself. I know you grew up in Nice, but what made you pick photography as a profession? What turned you into a paparazzo? And how on earth do you speak English so fluently?"

"That's a lot of questions in one go on a sleepy Sunday afternoon."

Flora propped her chin in her hands. "Pick just one of them for now, then."

"All right. I'll reply to your language question. I started learning English from an au pair my parents employed when I was four years old. She stayed with us for two years. Both my older brother and I were fluent by the time she left—children pick up a language without thinking. I kept the English up by watching English and American movies, and my parents subscribed to some of the BBC TV channels. Then, later, I spent some of my summer holidays as an exchange student in England and Scotland and finally did a degree course at the Sorbonne in Paris. It was there I discovered a love for photography and got a job as an apprentice to a very well-known fashion photographer. Then I branched out on my own. That's when I started to travel big time, wherever assignments took me. New York, Los Angeles, London…" He drew breath. "Was that enough information for now?"

"Yes. For now. I want to know about the women in your life, but we can do that later."

"Women? There have been a few. One or two serious ones and one in particular who broke my heart. But I recovered."

"I'm sure you did."

He put his hands under his head and peered at her. "What about you? What's your story? You're a bit of a mystery to me, Mademoiselle McKenna. You're very good at asking questions. How about answering a few for a change?"

"I suppose that's fair enough."

"It's very fair. So, tell me. Who is Flora McKenna? What made her come to this part of the world? What—or maybe I should say from whom is she running away?"

Flora sat up, turning her back to him. "I'm not…" She paused. She didn't like talking about herself. It took her back to painful, dark places. But if they were to become closer, to really get to know each other, she had to share some of her life story with him. "I do want to tell you. But this isn't the right place. It's too busy and public."

"It's getting late. People are leaving. So it's quieter here now. I'm not going to let you get away without telling me about yourself. We're not going home until you share some of what's inside that lovely blonde head."

Flora sat up and turned her back to him. "I had a normal childhood. My dad's an accountant, and my mum stayed at home with my brother and sister and me when we were very small. Then, when we were teenagers and old enough to look after ourselves after school, she went back to nursing. We lived in a semi-detached house in a suburb south of Dublin. When I left school, I trained as an estate agent. It took me four years to qualify." She drew breath.

Philippe tapped her back. "That's just your CV or résumé, as we say in France. I want to know more. I want to know why you picked that career."

Flora brushed sand from her toes. "I liked the idea of selling houses. And there was a huge property boom in Ireland when I trained. It was fascinating to learn the whole process. And I like people. The challenge of selling a house at the best price was also exciting."

"And you were good at it, I bet."

"I wasn't too bad."

"Then what happened?"

"What do you mean?"

"Something happened to you," Philippe said. "Someone broke your heart."

Flora turned to look at him. "What makes you say that?"

He shrugged. "Intuition. Vibes. There's something about you that makes me think you have something inside you won't let out. You have locked it up somewhere and you're afraid to look at it."

She was quiet for a long time, staring out to sea. Philippe lay there, saying nothing, obviously giving her a little space. She took a deep breath, somewhere between a sigh and a ragged sob.

"Yes. You're right."

"Tell me, Flora."

"All right. I'll tell you."

He sat up and put his arm around her. His skin against hers was comforting and created the closeness she needed at that moment.

"He cheated on me," she said. "Betrayed me."

"You were married?"

"No. Engaged."

"And he cheated on you with another woman? *Quel con!*"

"Yes. And then he did something worse."

"What?"

"He died."

* * *

Like a black wave that threatened to engulf her, it all came back to her as she started to tell Philippe what happened. She had to stop and close her eyes and swallow the big lump in her throat before she continued. Images and memories bubbled up to the surface from that place deep inside where she had locked up her feelings.

"His name was Matt," she said when she could speak. "We met at a party. He was older than me by about five years. Very handsome and fun. He seemed so sophisticated, with his own business and a flat in South Dublin." She turned and looked at Philippe. "Ballsbridge, a very posh neighbourhood."

"I know where it is. So you fell in love?"

"Yes," she whispered. "I thought he had too. We had a fantastic relationship for about a year, and then we got engaged. We started to save up to buy a house. We set up a joint account, which turned out to be a very stupid thing to do."

"I can guess the rest."

Flora shivered in her swimsuit, as the evening breeze ruffled her hair. Philippe put her shirt over her shoulders. "We can go, if you want. It's getting a little cool."

Flora pulled the shirt tight around her. "It's not the cool air that makes me shiver. I don't want to leave until you know." She buried her toes in the sand. "I can make it short, as you seem to have guessed the whole scenario anyway."

Philippe sat up and tightened his arms around her. "He stole the money?"

"Not technically, of course, but yes, he took all the money. He said that he had to pay back a short-term loan and that he'd put it back in the account as soon as he could. We had this long phone conversation about it, and then he said he had something he wanted to tell me in person. So I said I'd wait for him in my flat. He was on a business trip to Cork and was driving back that day. But he never arrived. He was killed in a pile-up on the motorway only a few hours after we spoke."

"So he died just after he took the money?"

Flora nodded. "Yes. And he was on his way to tell me he was in love with someone else. I found out at the funeral. *She* was there. Crying. Acting like some kind of widow. She said that he'd told her he was breaking up with me and that he'd come into some money so they could—" Flora stopped.

Without a word, Philippe pulled her close to him. She

buried her face in his chest, her eyes closed, the pain as sharp as that day, the day of the funeral. And for the first time since it happened two years earlier, she was able to cry. The tears came slowly at first, as if squeezed out of a rock, but once the floodgates opened, she was unable to stop. She pulled away after a while, embarrassed and bewildered, wondering if she was making a show of herself and him. But the beach was deserted, a few seagulls their only audience. At the far end of the beach she could see windsurfers pulling their boards up onto the sand, but they weren't close enough to notice what was going on.

Philippe wiped away her tears with his thumb. "Are you okay?"

Flora nodded, drying her face with a towel, rough with sand. "Fine. It felt good to cry. I didn't even do that at the funeral. I was too paralysed with shock and disbelief."

"Did you talk to that woman? I mean, did you ever find out why he did what he did?"

"Yes. Not at the funeral but afterwards. I caught up with her when she was about to get into her car. I was shaking, not with sorrow but rage. I couldn't take it out on him, so I let her have it instead. I called her all sorts of names. God, it makes me cringe when I think about how I behaved." Flora put her hands over her eyes as if to blot out the memory.

Philippe removed her hands and held them tight. "Nobody could blame you for being angry."

Flora leaned her forehead against his chest. "I was furious with him for dying, for not letting me punish him for what he did. *She* said he was tired of me because I was too bossy. I could tell she was the submissive type—tiny, busty, with long, curly, black hair. She looked like the perfect little wife." She pulled away and looked at Philippe. "Am I too bossy?"

Philippe brushed her hair away from her face. "No. Just bossy enough. You're clever, beautiful and very special."

"Oh." Flora sat back on her heels. "Thank you. You know,

it made me realise how *dependent* a woman is on a man she's in love with."

He nodded. "You're right. It's different for men. I don't think we feel as betrayed when that sort of thing happens. I've had a few affairs but not in the same way. Except that one time. But it wasn't meant to be. I've never really met a woman I wanted to spend more than a couple of weeks with. Until now," he added, touching her cheek.

Flora sat up. "Can we stop this now? I think I want to put all that back inside and lock it up again. I want to move forward."

Philippe smiled. "Me too." He got to his feet and started to gather up beach blankets, towels and the remains of their picnic. "Time to get going. We could have dinner in that little pizzeria across the road from the beach, if you feel like it?"

"Sounds like a good idea, if they don't mind a lot of sand on their floor."

"We'll clean ourselves up as much as we can. I'm sure they're used to a little bit of sand. We can sit outside, anyway. It's a warm evening."

Flora knew his chatter was a way of turning her mind away from the sadness. She slowly returned to the present and managed to pull herself together. The past was the past and the present was a lot better. She busied herself with getting dressed and tidying her hair. "I can't go to a restaurant looking as if I've been pulled through a hedge backwards," she joked.

"You look fine to me," Philippe said. "We both look a little untidy, but it's not exactly *La Colombe d'Or.*"

Flora stiffened. "Let's not go there, okay?"

Philippe nodded. "You still hate what I do, don't you?"

"With every fibre of my body," she replied with as much feeling as she could muster.

His face fell. "We need to talk about this."

Flora was going to reply but was interrupted by a tap on her shoulder. Startled, she he twirled around to come face to face with Ross.

"Hi, there," he said, shifting from foot to foot. "I saw you from a distance but wasn't sure it was you."

Flora smiled. His arrival diffused the tension, and his friendly smile pulled her out of the gloom. "Hi, Ross. It's great to see you. Good day on the waves?"

"Yup. Amazing north-westerly today, very steady with no sudden gusts. I could have gone all the way to Corsica on this wind." He nodded at Philippe and held out his hand. "Hi, I'm Ross. Ross Fitzgerald."

Philippe shook his hand. "Philippe Belcourt. So, you're a friend of Flora's?"

Ross nodded. "Yes. We met when I bought a house through the agency she works for."

Philippe's eyebrows rose. "Really? Which house?"

"The one on the hill," Ross replied. "A beautiful Bauhaus-inspired villa built in the nineteen thirties."

Philippe looked at Flora. "Was that the one we were talking about? Les Temps Heureux?"

"That's the one," Ross replied, before Flora had a chance to say anything.

"Beautiful house," Philippe said with an odd look at Flora. "But it needs a lot of work to get it habitable again, I think."

"Tell me about it," Ross laughed. "It's taken like forever, but I've nearly finished doing it up now."

Philippe studied Ross with more interest. "That can't have been cheap. Buying the house alone must have cost you a couple of million."

Ross laughed, his teeth white against his tanned face. "Yeah, it took quite a bit out of the wallet."

"I'm sure it did. So, what do you do for a living?" Philippe enquired casually.

"I rob banks," Ross said.

Philippe laughed, but there was a gleam of suspicion in his eyes. "You've been very successful at that, I take it."

"So far, yes." Ross winked at Flora. "Hey, I'd better get going. I've invited some of the windsurfer gang up to the house. Must see what there is in the fridge to feed them. Daisy and that other woman from the agency will be there."

"Who?" Flora asked. "You mean Iris?"

"Yeah, that's the one. She came down to the beach one evening, so I invited her. She seemed a little sad and lonely."

"Iris looked sad and lonely?" Flora said, realising he was right. Iris had never been particularly friendly and had never said anything about her personal life. Maybe it was because she had problems. Ross was more astute than she realised. There was more to him than that broad smile and puppy-like demeanour. But maybe he knew more about being lonely than anyone.

"Why don't you come, too, if you're free?" Ross suggested.

"Uh, maybe another time," Flora said. "I'm tired and I have an early start tomorrow. Not really in the mood for partying."

"Okay." Ross started to walk away. "Maybe another time. Nice to meet you, Philippe." He turned and jogged across the beach, jumped over the low wall, got into his jeep and drove off.

Philippe looked thoughtfully at the green jeep disappearing between the umbrella pines toward Cap d'Antibes. "Interesting. I could have sworn—"

"What?" Flora snapped, cursing herself for having introduced Ross to him.

Philippe shrugged. "Oh, nothing. Just a feeling I have."

"What kind of feeling?"

"That I've seen him somewhere before."

Chapter 15

"The operation was successful," the surgeon, still in scrubs, said to Chantal.

She rose from the chair in the waiting room. "Successful? What does that mean?"

He took off his cap. "Just that. We removed the tumour and the patient's comfortable. We'll have the result of the biopsy later today, but I'm confident it's benign."

"So what happens now? Can I see him?"

"Not yet. He will be kept under sedation until tomorrow, and then he'll come round slowly. We need you to be there when he wakes up. He'll be confused at first, maybe even frightened. We don't want him to be stressed, so your presence will calm him."

"Thank you. But…" Her knees weak, Chantal sank down on her chair again, staring at the surgeon.

He looked a little tired and worn, as if he got little sleep and was constantly in demand, but his eyes were friendly and his smile warm. "Please, don't worry, Madame. Your husband will be fine. He's strong physically which is a great help. But the road to his mental recovery will be long and difficult. He'll have a certain amount of memory loss."

"Memory loss? You mean he won't remember me?"

The surgeon sat down on the chair beside Chantal's. "I'm sure he'll know who you are. But he might not remember the time during which he was suffering from dementia. So he'll have no recollection of the past years."

"I see." Chantal shook her head and frowned, trying to understand. "So he'll have no more dementia? And it will seem to him as if he's been asleep for three years?"

The surgeon nodded. "Yes. That's what we think will happen. One thing I wanted to ask you, though, is if it would be possible for him to go to a private nursing home that specialises in rehabilitating patients with this kind of medical history. But it's quite expensive, and the French National Health Service only covers a small part of the cost."

"Yes, well…I think so. I've come into some money recently from the sale of a property. Where is this nursing home?"

"In Switzerland. It's run by a religious order, but the medical staff are the best in Europe. He'd get the very best rehabilitation, physiotherapy, speech therapy, cognitive training and of course, counselling. It would be the best and quickest way to a full recovery."

"Full recovery?" Chantal said as if to herself. Jean would be back to what he was. How would that feel? Could they go back to what they had before? And what about Gabriel?

The doctor rose and patted her shoulder. "Yes. Things will get a lot better. You'll have your husband back, body and soul. I'll get some more information for you and have the physiotherapist talk you through everything. But first things first. We'll have to keep a close eye on him for a couple of days at least. Don't worry, Madame, we'll look after him very well."

Just as the surgeon left, Chantal's phone rang. She peered at the name on the screen. Gabriel.

"*Bonjour, mon amour*," he said. "I miss you. How's Paris?"

"I haven't seen much of it. I've been in this hospital most of the time."

"How's your husband?"

His deep voice made her heart skip a beat. Oh to be with him again. To be in his arms and hear his voice, touch his face.

"He…" she started. "He's just come out of surgery. The doctors are hopeful he'll make a full recovery. Like he was before he became ill. It feels like a miracle, but it's true."

There was silence at the other end.

"Gabriel? Are you there? I said—"

"I heard. Good news for him, of course. But this…well, it'll change things between us, no?"

"Yes," she whispered.

"But let's not worry about that now. The important thing for you right now is to be with him and help him."

"Yes," she said again. "I'm sorry, Gabriel."

"Please," he begged. "Don't ever say sorry. We had our time. It might be over. Or not. We don't know. Let's just remember our love and be happy we had it. I'll always love you, Chantal."

Hot tears welled up in Chantal's eyes. "I'll always love you, too, Gabriel. Will you be all right?"

"I'll keep busy. I have my exhibition coming up and that will demand a lot of work."

"I'm sorry I can't be there."

"You will be. In nearly every painting. And forever in my heart. Goodbye, *mon amour*."

"*Adieu*," she said, knowing it could be the last time they spoke. They would never see each other again except at a distance. "*Adieu, mon coeur*."

* * *

"What's the story with Iris?" Flora asked the next morning as she and Daisy opened the office and prepared for the day ahead.

Daisy placed a stack of brochures on the small display table by the window. "What do you mean? What story?"

"What's going on in her life? I've never spoken to her

much except about work. Just curious really, but Ross said something about her being sad and lonely."

Daisy shrugged. "Not much of a story, really. She's a single mother and her son has a medical problem. So her life isn't exactly a dream come true. She was married to a Frenchman, and then he died before her son was born. She stayed here because his mother lived in the area. But she died some time ago. I suppose she'll go back to the UK eventually if she finds a good job there."

Flora went to gather up the morning's post from the doormat. "Oh. And I thought she came from a posh family."

"Posh but poor. Her dad was some kind of country squire, and she went to one of those high-class boarding schools. But then her dad died and the estate went to a cousin. Iris ended up with very little. I think her mother's living in a cottage on the estate or something. Runs a garden centre."

Flora stopped in her tracks. "Doesn't sound like a great life." How sad. And Iris was so pretty, with her gamine looks, short dark hair and petite frame. She was a little snippy at times and had never been very friendly, but her life story explained her lack of joie de vivre. Things couldn't have been easy for her. "How old's her little boy?"

"Two," Daisy said. The baby was born prematurely and has had no end of medical problems as a result. Something to do with his heart, I think. That, added to her grief for her husband, must have been such a burden to live with. Iris has been struggling with all of that."

"It must be very tough."

"It sucks," Daisy agreed and sat down behind the desk, logging in to her computer.

"Funny how Ross noticed how sad she is straightaway."

Daisy nodded. "Ross is a good guy. And Iris really enjoyed herself last night. I've never seen her so happy. Took years off her. She should really try to get out more often." Daisy glanced out the window. "But shh. Here she is now."

Flora nodded and flicked through the envelopes in her hand. She greeted Iris with a friendly 'good morning' and went into her office, her mind full of what Daisy had just told her. What a hard life Iris had. It must have been difficult to be friendly and cheerful with all of that going on. It couldn't do any harm to spend some time getting to know her better. Maybe invite her to have lunch later?

She forgot all about it when the phone rang and she heard Philippe's voice. He wanted to go away with her for the weekend. Not to somewhere fancy but for a drive to a hidden little village beyond St Tropez.

"Bormes le Mimosas," he said. "Have you been there?"

"No. Not yet."

"Lovely drive now that the tourist season's nearly over."

"I can't believe it's nearly September. How time has flown since we met."

"I know. Must go. I'm working on another photo shoot today. You'd approve. We're taking publicity stills for a movie that's coming out in December. This time, the celebrities are willing subjects."

"I'm glad to hear it," Flora retorted. "Much better to have their blessing, isn't it?"

"I don't care about *their* blessing. I only want yours."

Flora smiled. "You have it. For now. Are you going to embark on a more acceptable career path?"

"And behave?" He laughed. "I will for now. But don't expect me to turn into a saint."

"That would be a miracle."

"It would. I have to go. But just so you know I have bad intentions, I'll book a room at the little hotel in Bormes. The chaste dates are over, my sweet."

"And thank God for that," Flora whispered and hung up.

* * *

Getting to know Iris better proved to be a challenge. She accepted the invitation to lunch, but once they were seated at a table in the small bistro around the corner, she picked at her salad and only gave monosyllabic replies to Flora's questions.

"How about a glass of wine?" Flora suggested in desperation, hoping a little alcohol would loosen Iris up enough to engage in conversation.

Iris hesitated and looked as if she was about to say no but then said, "Yes, why not? Getting drunk with the boss might be good for my career."

"A small glass of wine's hardly going to make either of us drunk," Flora said. She gestured to a waiter and ordered a small carafe of rosé.

Iris shrugged. "I suppose."

Flora's patience ran out. "Oh, come on, Iris, why are you so sour? I know you don't have an easy life but is that my fault?"

Iris looked at her coldly for a full minute. "Is that my fault?" she mimicked. "Of course not, darling. It's nobody's fault that I have a shitty life, I know that. But watching others swanning around playing the manager and then slowly destroying an agency Chantal spent years trying to build up doesn't help. Not to mention riding around the Riviera in expensive cars with some rich playboy, enjoying a lifestyle I could never be a part of. To watch the sun shine in through the windows and see all those people on holiday without a care in the world, while I struggle to keep food on the table and pay medical bills for my son. Not to mention the cancer scare I had a couple of weeks ago, which was no fun, believe me. The lump turned out to be benign, but it was scary as hell all the same. So, no, my life isn't easy nor will it be in the foreseeable future."

Taken aback, not so much by the words, but the bitter tone with which they were spoken, Flora stared at Iris. "I had no idea. I'm so sorry, Iris. That's very hard for you."

"That's putting it mildly." Iris poured some wine from the carafe the waiter had just put on their table into her glass. She held it up. "Here's to life and happiness and all that crap." She drained the wine in one go and got up. "I'd better get back to the office. Daisy will probably have done a bunk and gone windsurfing with her millionaire friends." She pulled a twenty-euro note from the front pocket of her shirt and threw it on the table. "Here's my part of the lunch."

"But it was my treat," Flora stammered. "I wanted to take you to lunch."

"I don't accept charity. See you in the office." Iris walked swiftly out of the bistro, leaving Flora sitting there, stunned and appalled.

* * *

"Do you want to go to a gallery opening?" Daisy asked Flora the following evening as they closed up shop.

"Where?" Flora asked.

"It's a small gallery near the harbour. Bruno got an invitation, but he can't go so he gave it to me. Said I could take a friend or two. Very select. It's a famous painter in these parts. And he's a bit of a hunk too." Daisy winked. "We might even get to meet him."

"Who is he?"

"Gabriel Sardou. You might not have heard of him, but he's very well-known and also a bit of a celebrity on the Riviera. I think there are two of his paintings in Chantal's office."

"Oh yes, that's right. Lovely landscapes. If that's the artist, I'd love to go."

"Great. We could grab a bite to eat afterwards. Apparently this is a new departure for him. He has done a series of paintings of the Bay of Angels at different times of the day or something. I read about it in Nice Matin. They should sell for millions."

"You could ask Ross. Maybe he'd like something for the house?"

"I don't know if he'd want to go," Daisy replied with a glance at Iris, who was rapidly typing something into her computer, her earphones stuck in her ears. Daisy lowered her voice. "He said he thought someone has been spying on him. Could be that his secret's been shot."

"He's told you about—?"

Daisy nodded. "Yes. And now he could be exposed."

"Oh, no," Flora murmured. "That would be awful."

"Yes, terrible," Daisy agreed. "If his identity's revealed, a photo of him could fetch a very large sum."

"Not to mention his life would be wrecked," Flora added. "Has he told you about—"

Daisy nodded, her face solemn. "Yes. Sad story."

"Yeah. Poor little boy. He'd better lay low for a while and stay put in case there's some kind of alert among the media people."

"That's what he said. I hope your Philippe doesn't get wind of this."

"He won't if I have anything to do with it," Flora said grimly, remembering how Philippe had reacted to Ross.

Daisy didn't look convinced. "Are you sure? Not even during a little pillow talk?"

Flora felt her face flush. "Absolutely not."

"Good." Daisy turned to Iris who had stopped typing. "Iris, do you want to come to a gallery opening tonight? Could be fun. Free wine and nibbles, I'm told."

Iris shrugged. "Yes, why not? I could do with some culture. I'll see if I can get a babysitter." She glanced at Flora. "Sorry about the hostility yesterday. I was feeling grumpy."

"No problem," Flora muttered, not quite ready to forgive and forget.

Daisy looked from Iris to Flora. "This promises to be a jolly evening, girls. Could we hold the bitching till later?"

"Fine by me," Flora said.

Iris nodded. "Of course."

"Brilliant," Daisy said. "Let's close up and get going. We can walk to the gallery—it's not that far."

Daisy led the way through the narrow streets, wobbling on the cobblestones in her high heels, Flora and Iris following. The evening sun, slowly sinking behind the headland of Cap d'Antibes was still warm, and the light wind carried a smell of salt and seaweed from the nearby harbour. The gallery was in a stone-faced house in an alley just beyond the marina. There was a poster outside, announcing the exhibition of new work by Gabriel Sardou. 'The many faces of The Bay of Angels', the poster announced above a photo of one of the paintings.

Daisy stopped to look at it. "Lovely, even on a poster. And look, there's a woman there, just at the edge, turning her face away to look at the view. He doesn't usually have people in his paintings."

Flora looked at the poster. The picture with the deep-blue sweep of the bay and the buildings lining it was truly wonderful. And in one corner, the profile of a woman, her hair blowing across her face made it feel as if the bay was being viewed through her eyes. There was something familiar about that profile, the hair and the set of the jaw. Flora kept staring at the picture, until Daisy pulled at her.

"Come on, let's go in and see the paintings. That photo's only a copy."

"The real thing will be even more spectacular," Iris said.

Flora nodded and followed Iris and Daisy inside where she was instantly captivated by the large canvases, hung in a series according to the time of day. And the woman was in each painting in different ways. In one, there was just the tip of a shoulder and a strand of dark hair, but her presence was still strong.

"Must be his muse or something," Daisy said.

"Or his mistress," Iris mumbled, walking ahead, looking at the final painting in the series, where the mystery woman had turned her head and was looking at them, her face half hidden by her hair falling across her face.

"Look at those eyes," Daisy whispered to Flora. "Like blue ice. They remind me of someone. What about you?"

Flora stopped and stared, as it suddenly dawned on her. "Yes. Of course. It's Chantal."

Chapter 16

"Shh, not so loud," Daisy hissed. "Someone might hear you."

Flora looked around the nearly empty gallery. The only occupants of the large room were a woman filling glasses of wine at a table and a tall thin man talking into his phone beside her.

"There's hardly anyone here. We arrived a little ahead of the opening time."

"Yeah, but if Chantal's having an affair with the artist, I'm sure she wouldn't want it shouted to the whole world," Daisy argued.

"Can't believe she's having an affair," Flora said.

"If that's *him* over there, on the phone, can't say I blame her," Iris muttered.

"Her husband suffers from some kind of mental illness," Daisy added in a low voice. "It must be hard to deal with.

Appalled, Flora looked at Daisy. "I had no idea. She always looks so cool and chic and in control. I thought he had just had an accident. God, Daisy, why didn't you tell me?"

Daisy shrugged. "Not something I felt I could share. Chantal told me about it once in confidence. She's very strong, you know."

"She must be." Flora walked further into the room as a big group of people arrived at once behind her, all looking in awe at the paintings and murmuring their appreciation to each other. She moved along the wall and admired the rest of the paintings in the collection, all with the same theme, The Bay of Angels in different lights and from different points of view. She glanced back at the first four canvases and realised something else was familiar, apart from the woman she was now sure was Chantal. The view of the bay was exactly as she had seen it that day with Ross from the window of the room that was locked up. The house, Ross's house, called Les Temps Heureux, must have belonged to Chantal.

She pushed through the now-thick throng to have another look and bumped into someone pushing through in the other direction.

"Oh, *excusez-moi*," she exclaimed as she noticed he had spilled a few drops of wine onto his white shirt.

The tall man looked at his shirt, then down at her. "*C'est pas grave*. It's an old shirt." He brushed his dark floppy hair out of his eyes and smiled. "Sorry, I didn't look where I was going. I was trying to get to the art critic from *Le Figaro*. She wants to interview me for her article."

"You're Gabriel Sardou?" Mesmerised by the combination of his charisma, good looks and amazing eyes, she was suddenly stuck for words.

He nodded. "Yes, that's me."

"Your paintings are wonderful."

"Thank you. I'm glad you like them." He looked closer at her. "You're English?"

"No, Irish."

"I see. You speak very good French but there is a little accent."

"More than a little," Flora said.

"You're here on holiday?"

"No. I work here in Antibes. In an estate agency called *Agence du Soleil*. You might have heard of it," she said without thinking and then realised that of course, he must have.

His expression changed. "Yes. I know where it is. But

if you excuse me…" He smiled and sidled away, hurrying across the room to join a woman wielding a notepad and pen.

"You talked to…*him*?" Daisy gasped beside her. "What did he say?"

Flora sighed. "He said I was the most beautiful woman he had ever seen, and he wants me to pose naked for him in his studio tonight."

Daisy's eyes were like saucers. "He did?"

Flora laughed. "Nah, just in my dreams."

Daisy pushed at her. "And mine. Gee, that guy's so hot. Chantal's a lucky bitch."

"Yes, but I'm sure there's a lot more to it than we think. A lot of sadness and conflict."

Iris joined them. "It's getting crowded. How about going to get something to eat? There's a little place around the corner that does Provençal cuisine—very cheap. The ratatouille is delicious."

Daisy's phone rang. She looked at the screen. "It's Ross. Shall I ask him to join us?"

"Yes, good idea," Iris replied. "Please tell him we'd love some male company."

"Okay," Daisy said with a sideways glance and a wiggle of her eyebrows at Flora.

The arrangements were made. Daisy put away her phone, took one last look at Gabriel Sardou surrounded by a crowd of well-wishers at the far end of the gallery and led the way through the door and down the street.

Flora tagged along behind the others, her mind full of the paintings she had seen. She jumped as someone tapped her shoulder. It was Gabriel Sardou.

"*Excusez moi*," he said, smiling apologetically. "I meant to talk to you before you left. I wanted to ask you…are you the young woman who's running Chantal's agency?"

Flora nodded. "Yes, I am. Why?"

He shrugged. "Oh, no reason. I just thought…you might have heard…about her husband, I mean. How is he?"

"I'm not sure I should tell you," she started. "But as I've seen the paintings and put everything together, I understand your connection with her."

He pushed his fingers through his hair. "You do?"

She felt her face flush. "Not really…but I recognised her in the paintings. And I noticed that some of the views were from a house, where—" She stopped. It was all assumption, and there was no real proof her suspicions were correct. "Forgive me. I didn't want to be nosy. I shouldn't have jumped to conclusions. That woman might not even be her."

He looked thoughtfully at her. "She is and she isn't. I mean, she inspired me, but the woman in the painting is more like a spirit—or a symbol of all women. The goddess, the spirit of femininity, if you like."

"That's a lovely idea. I did feel there was something spiritual about the woman."

He nodded, looking pleased. "Yes, that's it. I'm glad it made you feel that way." He paused. "So…can you tell me anything about her? Is she well? Is her husband…?"

Flora met his eyes, so full of sorrow it made her heart ache for him—and her. They must have loved each other deeply, knowing it was hopeless. How sad. She cleared her throat. "All I can tell you is that Chantal's husband's recovering well. It's going to take a long time. But the doctors are very hopeful. She sounded tired but quite happy."

He sighed. "Good. Thank you."

"It's good news, isn't it?"

He nodded. "Yes. For him and maybe for her too. But for me? It's the end." He turned on his heel and walked swiftly back to the gallery

Minutes later, the three women were seated at a table near the window in the crowded restaurant, overlooking the narrow alley and the facades of the old houses. The smell of garlic and herbs permeated the room, and Flora sniffed hungrily, her stomach rumbling. She grabbed a menu.

"I'll have everything. I could eat a horse, provided it's cooked with these wonderful spices."

When the waitress arrived at their table, they all ordered ratatouille and grilled lamb cutlets, asking to have a place set for Ross, whom they could see wandering up the alley, wearing a baseball cap and sunglasses.

"Hi," he said when he had managed to push through the crowd at the bar. "Thanks for inviting me. I was getting cabin fever, staying at home the past couple of days."

"I think you can relax now," Daisy said. "Take off those shades and the cap. Nobody here has any idea or is even mildly interested in who you might be. They're all stuffing their faces with ratatouille."

Ross looked around at the eating, drinking, chatting crowd and took off his sunglasses and cap. He sat down beside Daisy. "Yeah, you're probably right. It was just that I got spooked by an article in an American tabloid. There was a photo of me taken at my dad's funeral. Don't know how they got it. But it was very sharp and a good likeness. That and the report in The Daily Telegraph a while back that I was seen in Cannes by someone who knew me might start a buzz."

Iris stared at Ross. "Who are you, then? I thought you were just a poor bloke who won a zillion dollars in the lottery."

"Uh, not really," Ross started. He looked around and lowered his voice. "I know I can trust you as much as Flora and Daisy, so…"

Iris met his gaze. "So?"

Ross took the napkin from his lap. "Has anyone got a pen?"

Daisy dug in her handbag. "No, but you can use my lipstick."

Ross scribbled something on the napkin with Daisy's lipstick and handed it to Iris. "That's who I am."

Iris squinted at the napkin. "Joseph—Christ!" She looked at Ross with respect in her eyes. "You're *him*," she whispered.

"Yeah, that's why he's so good at windsurfing," Daisy joked. "He walks on water."

Ross laughed. "That's why everyone wants a piece of me."

Iris kept looking at Ross. "Unbelievable."

"I know," Ross said. "But I'm trying to forget all that. So I'm not *him* anymore. I'm me, Ross Fitzgerald, okay?" There was steel in his eyes as he looked at Iris.

She nodded and dropped her gaze. "Of course." She gathered her handbag. "I'm going to the loo. Excuse me for a moment."

Flora looked at Iris weaving her way through the crowded restaurant to the ladies' room. "Are you sure that was a good idea? Iris can be a little hostile at times."

"Yeah, she's a bit of a bitch," Daisy said. "But an honest bitch. She would never squeal on Ross."

"I'm sure she wouldn't," Ross agreed. "She might be sour sometimes but she's not a loose cannon. I'm pretty sure of that."

Daisy glanced at Flora. "I know of only one person who might squeal. But as long as he's kept in the dark, we're pretty safe. Right, Flora?"

* * *

Jean smiled at Chantal. "It's you." He sat up against the pillows and stretched out his hand. "Chantal. My wife. At least I know that."

She took his hand. "How do you feel?"

"Strange, as if I have been away for a long time on some kind of journey."

"What's your last memory?"

He squeezed her hand and looked thoughtful. "Nothing specific. But I feel as if I slipped slowly into a kind of sleep. And now I'm coming out of that sleep, and my memory is hazy and pale. There are shadows, bits of memory floating around." He shook his head. "I've been told I have to learn things all over again. I need to know what's been going on in the world while I was…away. And that I need therapy and training."

Chantal nodded. "Yes you do. I'm taking you to a clinic in Switzerland, where you can get the very best care and all kinds of therapy."

He looked suddenly frightened. "Switzerland? Will you come with me?"

"Of course. I'll stay with you while you're getting better."

He looked around the bare hospital room with its pale-green walls, grey linoleum floor and the window overlooking a concrete wall and breathed in the ether-laden air. "I'm looking forward to getting out of this soulless place."

"So am I," Chantal sighed. "Switzerland will be heaven after this."

His eyes focused on her, as if he had suddenly just realised she had a life, too. "And you, Chantal, where have you been these past years?"

"With you, of course," she said, tears welling up in her eyes. "Always with you."

He removed his hand. "I know that. But you must have had some kind of personal life. Work, friends…" He paused. "Maybe even love?"

She got up and walked to the window, staring out into that grey space so he wouldn't see her tears. His eyes were so knowing as if he had not only regained his mental capacities, but also some kind of second sight that could reach into her heart and mind. It frightened her.

"I've been away too," she said, hugging herself, trying to stop shivering.

"Have you returned?" Jean asked in a gentle voice.

Brushing away tears, she turned and looked at him. How fragile he was, how frightened and thin. His beautiful eyes gazed out of a gaunt face, and his once-luxurious brown hair lay flat against his skull. He had to get strong again. She had to give him back his life. She closed her eyes for a moment and tried to conjure up the image of Gabriel that last time they were together. But the image was blurred like a barely-there shadow. She opened her eyes again and looked at Jean across the expanse of grey linoleum.

"I'm on my way," she said.

* * *

"I lied," Philippe said as he drove up the winding road to Bormes les Mimosas. "I didn't book a room. I borrowed a house for the weekend, high in the hills above the village. It's just a small mas, quite primitive. We have to rough it a bit but it'll be worth it for the view."

"You crook," Flora said and pulled his hair. "I knew you were up to something. How did you know I liked camping?"

"You have that air about you. There's something wanton and wild about the way you look."

Flora laughed. "You mean the way my hair's always in a mess and I seem to forget to put on make-up?"

"I like that. You're a free spirit."

They slowed down as the road became nothing more than a dirt track and so narrow that the rough bushes brushed the sides of the car. They wobbled up another half mile or so and then Philippe stopped the car in front of a small wooden gate set in a high hedge. Flora could see a tiled roof above the vegetation. She looked up at the blue sky, breathed in the scent of thyme and pine and listened to the crickets and the cooing of doves.

"Heaven," she whispered as she caught sight of the sapphire blue sea far below them. "You brought me to heaven."

Philippe got out of the car. "You'll change your mind when you see the bathroom…or the lack of it. There's only an outdoor shower and a tiny toilet beside the kitchen."

Flora jumped out of the car. "I don't care. Who needs a bathroom when you have this?"

They unloaded their bags and walked through the gate, into a small garden, where roses and oleander grew in abundance, their colours vibrant against the pink stucco of the little house. The door was open. Flora kicked off her shoes and walked through a living room furnished with sofas and chairs, upholstered in colourful Provençal prints, and into a bright kitchen that had a view of the hills and the mountain range beyond. There was a box of fruit and vegetables on the counter and even some cheese wrapped in wax paper with a bottle of red wine and a still-warm baguette.

"Some fairy godmother has been here already," Flora remarked and pointed at the food.

"I asked to have it all delivered from the village," Philippe said. "But I need to go to the butcher for steaks, so we can have a barbeque on the terrace later."

"Perfect. I'm starving." Flora nipped a piece from the end of the baguette and put it in her mouth.

"You haven't seen the bedroom yet," Philippe said and opened a door off the living room. "It's the best part of the house."

"I knew you'd say that." Flora walked across the cool tiles of the living room and peered in. He was right. It was a lovely room with polished wooden floorboards and whitewashed walls hung with pictures and tapestries in vibrant colours. The large bed was covered in an exquisite quilt that echoed the bright prints of the living room, and the window, with its sheer lace curtains, overlooked the small terrace, the front garden and the breathtaking views of the sea below. The smell of roses mingled with freshly ironed sheets and the light breeze gently stirred the curtains. Flora padded across the floor, lay on the bed and closed her eyes. It was like stepping into a dream or some magic fairy tale. She could feel Philippe lie down beside her.

"Don't wake me up," she murmured. "I want this dream to last forever."

"Me too," Philippe whispered and took off his shirt.

She opened her eyes. He looked so young and oddly vulnerable, lying there, stripped to the waist. She ran a finger from his forehead, down his nose, chin and neck and stopped at the hollow of his throat.

"Can't be a dream," she murmured. "I can feel your stubble and your—"

His kiss silenced her, and his fingers undoing all the buttons of her silk blouse made her shiver. They hadn't made love since that first night, and the long period of chaste dating had made her want him more than ever. The heat and fervour of his kisses and the way he stripped off her clothes in a matter of seconds told her he felt the same. His warm skin against hers was like silk, his lips and hands ignited a fire neither of them could—or would—put out. Heart to heart, their limbs entwined, what followed was to Flora true lovemaking.

When it was over, he collapsed on top of her and let out a long sigh. She put her arms around him and pressed her mouth against his neck, breathing in the scent of his skin.

"*Je t'aime*," he said. "*Mon amour, ma belle, ma petite* Flora."

"*Moi aussi*," she replied. "I love you just as much. And I love it when you speak French to me."

"It's the language of love." He pulled away and looked deep into her eyes. "You couldn't possibly love me. How could you? I'm a rogue, a liar, a thief."

She laughed, knowing he was right, but not caring. "What does it matter? You haven't lied to me."

"That's true. I never lied to you. I just didn't tell you what I was up to."

"And when I found out..." She thought for a moment. Why had she reacted so strongly? Was it the fact that he was sneaking up on people during what should be private moments? Or that he made a lot of money from revealing their secrets to the press? "Oh, God, Philippe, I hate what you do. Can't you give it up? Make money some other way?"

He rolled onto his back, looking up at the ceiling. "Not yet. But maybe in time. I'm trying to break into advertising. You know, those big, glamorous photos of high-profile brands that are sold to every glossy magazine in the world. That makes a lot of money. I could even, if I'm lucky, get a contract with one of the really big magazines, like Paris Match or even Vanity Fair and be sent out to take shots of heads of state and royalty."

Flora pulled a corner of the quilt over her legs. "How would you do that?"

"First, I need an agent. I've submitted to two high-profile ones, and they'll get back to me next week. If either of them takes me on as a client, they'll start sending out my portfolio to advertising agencies and media groups. It'll take a while but I'm prepared to wait. If I succeed, it'll mean a new beginning, a whole new career."

Flora's heart sank. "And in the meantime—?" she asked, even though she knew the answer.

He stroked her cheek. "I'll be sneaking up on famous people, my darling. It's too lucrative to leave alone. But don't worry, I'll just shoot people you don't know."

"I don't know any cele—" she started. But then Ross popped into her mind. She could never reveal his real identity. And Gabriel. Very famous. His affair—if that's what it was—would have created quite a stir and cause a lot of pain for Chantal.

"You might know them but not be aware of their fame,"

Philippe said. "But I'd never go near any of your friends, and that's a promise."

"Okay," Flora mumbled. "I appreciate that."

"And in any case, the season here's nearly over, except for Nice and Monte Carlo. I'll go to Paris in a week or two. Maybe even to London for a bit."

"You're going away?" Flora asked, alarmed. "But we only just—"

He put his finger on her mouth. "Shh. Don't worry. It'll only be for short periods and only for the next few months. When I get myself an agent, I'll establish a base, depending on what kind of deal they can get me. Could be London or even New York. And if I move away, I want you to come with me."

She took his hand. "Come with you? You mean—?"

He kissed her cheek. "Yes. I want to live with you, *ma petite fleur*. I want you with me wherever I go."

"Me too," she said and snuggled closer to him. Being together was the most important thing at that moment, even if her own career didn't seem to be part of the equation for him. Those details could be sorted out later. "I hope we won't leave Antibes for good, though," she added. "I love living here."

"We can buy a little place, like this one, for breaks and holidays." He sat up. "But I'd better get to the butcher down in the village for those steaks. They close at five on Fridays." He patted her leg. "I'll just have a quick shower. Will you be all right here by yourself for a while?"

Flora stretched and smiled. "I'll be fine. I'll have a shower, too, and then I'll explore the garden."

"*Très bien.* I'll get something for dessert at the patisserie."

After Philippe had left, Flora got up. She found a towel hanging on a peg on the back of the bedroom door and with that wrapped around her, went out to the shower, which was in a small enclosure just off the terrace. The soft water trickling over her, she looked up at the sky just visible between the branches of a majestic umbrella pine above her and slowly washed herself all over with lavender soap. What could be more perfect than this? Mellow autumn sunshine, lavender soap, the air thick with the scent of pine and wild thyme, and the water, soft as silk, running down her body into the sandy soil. Primitive, yes, but at the same time sensual and serene.

Completely at peace with herself and her surroundings, Flora got dressed and went to the kitchen to put the groceries away. She opened the bottle of wine and poured herself a glass. It was a soft, mellow Bordeaux with undertones of blackberry and vanilla: perfect with the steaks later. When she had put away all the food in the tiny fridge, she took the glass with her and went out to the terrace to enjoy the view while she waited for Philippe. Hopefully, he wouldn't be long. It had been a while since she last ate and she was beginning to get hungry.

She had just sat down in one of the rickety rattan chairs when her phone rang inside. How annoying. Better let it ring and deal with it later. But maybe it was Philippe? Flora got up and ran to her handbag she had left in the living room. Slightly blinded by the sun, she tried to focus and finally found the bag, just as the phone stopped ringing. She looked up the missed call and recognised the number. Ross. What could he want? He knew she was away with Philippe for the weekend and wouldn't have disturbed her for just a chat. The phone rang again. Flora pressed the button to reply.

"Hi, Ross. What's up?"

"Flora, can you come over?"

"What? But I told you. I'm away for the weekend. Philippe and I are at this little house in Bormes les—"

"Shit, I forgot," Ross moaned. "I'm sorry. Forget it. Call me when you get back."

"No, please tell me what's wrong," Flora demanded,

alarmed by the panic in his voice. "I can tell you're upset. Philippe's gone down to the village to get something, so I'm on my own."

"It's…" He paused. "Have you seen this evening's *France Soir*?"

"No. I haven't read any newspaper today. I never read those tabloidy things, anyway. Why?" she asked, with an eerie feeling she knew what he was going to say.

"They've found me."

"They? Who?"

"The paparazzi or whatever they're called. There's a shot of me at the beach and another of me at the restaurant we were at after the art exhibition. With my real name and then that photo from my dad's funeral, just to compare. Great shots—very sharp and no mistaking it."

Flora's heart sank. "Holy mother," she whispered. "What are you going to do?"

"I don't know," Ross whimpered. "I'm stuck here, in the house for the moment. They haven't discovered where I live. The article mentions Cannes and St Tropez, so for the moment, I'm safe here."

"Shit," Flora said and got up. "Shit, shit, shit! Why did he have to do it?"

"Who?"

"Philippe, of course. Must have been him." She started to pace the length of the terrace. "And I *trusted* him," she said bitterly. "I believed his promise to not go near my friends. What a total eejit I've been."

"I…what are you going on about? What has Philippe got to do with this?"

"I never told you, probably because I didn't want to alarm you. But Philippe is one of *them*…a paparazzo, someone who sneaks up on famous people and takes their photo without their permission." Her anger and disappointment grew as she spoke. How could he have done this to Ross?

Had he no feelings? No respect for anyone? Now Ross's life was ruined. He would have to dodge the press for the rest of his life. Her legs like jelly, Flora sank down on the rickety chair again, the phone clamped to her ear. "What are you going to do?" she said to Ross.

"Dunno. For the moment, stay put in the house. Grow a beard. Dye my hair. Put on a hundred pounds and dress like a tramp." Ross let out a hollow laugh.

"I'll come over as soon as I can."

"No, I don't want to ruin your weekend."

"Are you kidding?" Flora said bitterly. "This weekend is shot to hell already. Along with the so-called relationship I was supposed to have had with that bastard."

"Gee, I'm sorry. I shouldn't have called."

"I'm so glad you did! It has opened my eyes to who he really is."

"What are you going to do?"

"I don't know. But I'll think of something. I'll keep you posted." She was about to hang up but changed her mind. "I'm really sorry about this, Ross."

"Not your fault. It was a disaster waiting to happen. Please don't blame yourself."

"I can't help it, but I do. Anyway…" Flora sighed. "I'll see you soon. Why don't you call Daisy? She'll get over to you a lot quicker than me."

"She's probably away on some romantic weekend with her boyfriend, too," Ross said bleakly.

"No, she's not. I think he's away. Go on. Call her."

"Okay. I will. See you soon."

Flora hung up with a feeling of doom. This was the end. It was happening again. Lies and deceit. Betrayal. She had a horrible sense of déjà vu. But this time, it would be different. This time she wouldn't be a victim. She would walk away with her head held high and her pride intact. No man would ever do this to her again. Her heart was breaking, but at the same time she looked forward to having it out with Philippe. He would finally have to tell her the truth.

Chapter 17

The clinic, twenty minutes' drive from Geneva, was more like a luxury hotel than a hospital or anything to do with health care. High in the foothills of the Alps, it had wonderful views of Lac de Genève and the surrounding countryside below. There was calm atmosphere there, in the soft autumn sunshine, and the air felt as if it had more oxygen than anywhere else. Chantal got out of the car to help Jean, but he was already standing outside, looking at the view and taking deep breaths.

"What an invigorating place," he said. "If this doesn't help me get back to life, nothing will." He turned to Chantal. "But it's quite expensive, no?"

Chantal smiled. "Yes, it costs a fortune. But don't worry. I just got the money for the sale of the house into my bank account, so there's plenty to meet the costs of everything."

He put his arm around her shoulders. "*Les Temps Heureux*. You sold it. My memory of it is very hazy but I know we were happy there. And it was your home. How sad that you had to sell it."

She sighed. "Yes, sad. But we couldn't afford to keep it. Better to let someone else be happy there than leave it empty or have to struggle to pay for the repairs. It was bought by a young man who's going to do it up. Perhaps he, in time, will have a family, and they'll be as happy as we were."

Jean turned away from the view and looked at her. "I'm

sorry to have to ask this but…why didn't we have children? I know we've been married for a long time, and I do remember a lot of that. But then I thought…no children. Was it my fault?"

"No," Chantal said, trying to keep the sadness out of her voice. "It wasn't. I got pregnant once, after years of trying, but I lost the baby. Then I had an infection and had to have a hysterectomy, so we couldn't even try again."

Jean nodded. "Yes, I remember that. But did we ever consider adoption?"

Chantal shrugged. "No. You didn't want to. By then we were used to life with just us."

He squeezed her shoulder. "I'm sorry."

She leaned closer against him. "Oh, it doesn't make me sad anymore. I don't think I was meant to be a mother. We were happy together and the agency was our baby, really."

The porter carried the luggage into the reception area. Chantal thanked him and turned to Jean. "Time to get you settled and organised. I'm staying at a small guesthouse nearby, just a few minutes from here." She pointed down the road they had just come up. "Look. That roof down there. It's a lovely chalet within easy walking distance. So I can come and be with you every day."

He looked in the direction she was pointing. "Looks nice."

His room was bright and airy and had the same views. Chantal helped him unpack. "The director of the clinic will see us after lunch. And then I'll go and check into the guesthouse and let you rest."

Jean turned from the bedside locker where he had just put some books and magazines. "I don't want you to stay there."

"What?" she exclaimed, alarmed. What was he saying? Was he getting confused again? "But there's nowhere else nearby, so I—"

He grabbed her arm and looked at her with desperation. "I don't know how to say this, my dearest Chantal. But I want you to leave me here and go. I want to be on my own for a while. To…to find myself, as the cliché goes. To get back to the life that stopped all those years ago. I have a feeling you had some kind of other life during that time, some liaison. Am I right?"

"How did you know?"

"I heard you talking on the phone with someone when I was in the hospital. You thought I was asleep."

"I…I…" she stammered. Unable to meet his probing eyes, she lowered her head. "Yes. I fell in love. With a younger man. Nobody knew. I know I was cheating on you but…"

Jean shook his head. "I don't see how you could feel like that. I wasn't there. My mind was a blank. I had become some kind of zombie. You cared for me, but you had no emotional life, nobody to love you and appreciate your beauty. How could I reproach you for turning to someone else?"

"I felt guilty, though. But at the same time not. It was so strange. Being with him was like being on holiday for a while, and yes, I loved him." Tears seeped out of the corners of her eyes and she tried to blink them away.

"And now?" he asked, his voice hoarse. "You still love him?"

She lifted her tear-stained face to look at him. "Yes, I still love him, in a way. But I love you too, Jean. I love you with all my heart, and I want to help you back to life. Oh, I'm so confused."

He put a finger under her chin and tilted her face closer to his. "Go, then, Chantal. Go and find yourself, too. I'll be here if you want to come back. And if you don't…" He shrugged. "There's nothing I can do about it."

She closed her eyes, unable to bear the deep pain she saw in his. Then she opened them again and looked at him, knowing what he said was true. She had to go back and face

Gabriel. Find out how she felt about him and Jean. Only then could she carry on with her own life.

* * *

Flora's stomach churned as she heard Philippe's car approach. This was it. The showdown. She was armed with the front page of *France Soir* on her iPhone and ready to stick it in his face when he arrived. Anticipating the approaching storm with trepidation, she watched as Philippe jumped out of the car with the small package of meat and a bunch of flowers.

"Ciao, bella," he chanted and ran to her side, crushing her to his chest and planting a hot kiss on her lips.

Flora tore away and held out her hand with her phone. "Stop it right there. I want you to explain this."

Confused, he frowned and backed away. "What's wrong?"

"What's *wrong*?" she shouted, tears of rage welling up. "I'll tell you what's wrong. You did it, didn't you? You betrayed one of my friends despite swearing you wouldn't."

Philippe dropped the flowers and they tumbled onto the tiles in a colourful mess. "What are you talking about?"

"*This*!" Flora shouted, sticking the phone in his face. "First page news in the evening's *France Soir*. 'Heir to the Herbert-Rothschild fortune discovered on the French Riviera," she quoted. "And the photos tell the rest of the story." She looked at him through her tears. "How could you?"

Philippe grabbed the phone from Flora and looked at the screen. His eyes widened in shock. "But that's your friend—what's his name…Ross? You mean he really is… Joseph Charles Herbert Jr? *Nom d'un chien, c'est incroyable!*"

Flora tore the phone back from him. "Oh, yeah, great acting, I must say. How much did you get for those pictures? Ten thousand each? You must have sneaked up on him at the beach when he came back from windsurfing. But how did you find us at the restaurant? Did you follow me there?" Breathing hard, she waited for his response.

Philippe took a step closer. "Flora. It wasn't me. I didn't know anything about this. And even if I did, I'd never have done it. Please believe me."

His eyes were so earnest and his pleading voice so beguiling, Flora nearly relented. Maybe he was telling the truth? Maybe someone else took those photos? But nobody except Philippe knew the world of the jet set enough to make the connection between Ross and his real persona. And hadn't he said just recently he had a feeling he had seen Ross before? It had to be him, and in that case, his continued deceit was worse than if he had confessed. Betrayed again. He was just like Matt. But this time she wouldn't allow it to destroy her. She would walk away and leave him standing there, looking like the cheat and liar he was.

"I don't believe you," she said and blindly groped for her bag. "I'm leaving. I can't stand a minute more with you."

"Where are you going?"

"Anywhere away from you. I'll walk to the village and catch a bus back to Antibes."

His eyes hardened. "*Très bien.* It's a good twenty-minute walk to the village. The bus only goes from there every hour, so you'll have a long wait if you miss it."

"I don't care."

"Fine." He picked up the packet of meat that had fallen on top of the flowers. "I'll make myself some dinner. Goodbye, Flora."

They looked at each other for a loaded minute, and Flora felt a thousand words pass between them. Something really important and good was being destroyed. But who was at fault? Her heart breaking into a thousand pieces, she hitched her bag onto her shoulder and walked out of the lovely little garden. Tears streaming down her face, she trundled down the dusty road to the village, every step marking her growing distance away from Philippe.

The village was quiet, the streets empty, echoing with the cooing of doves and the odd chirping of a bird. The setting sun infused the main street with a golden hue, and Flora could smell meat grilling on a barbeque nearby. Her stomach rumbling, she remembered she hadn't eaten anything since lunch, except that small piece of bread just before Ross had called.

The noise of a car coming down the street at speed interrupted her thoughts, and she was shocked to see Philippe coming into view, driving like a lunatic towards her.

"Flora!" he shouted as he slowed down. "Flora, please listen to me!"

She was about to reply and take a step towards him, but the bus coming the other way made her retreat. As if in slow motion, she watched helplessly as the bus slammed into Philippe's car and turned it over, throwing him onto the pavement.

* * *

"He's alive," she heard someone say, as she stood there, paralysed with shock. She didn't know who had called the ambulance, but there it was with two paramedics tending to Philippe. The bus driver was talking to a policeman, whose motorbike was parked at the kerb, lights flashing and radio shouting with voices nobody answered.

"Whose fault was it?" the policeman asked the bus driver.

Flora held up a shaking hand, like a small child at school. "Mine," she croaked. "It was all my fault."

The policeman looked at her as if he had only just noticed her. "You, Mademoiselle? But you are not in any vehicle. How could it be your fault?"

"I distracted him," she said.

"Distracted who?"

"Him." She pointed at Philippe who, wearing a neck brace, was being lifted onto a stretcher. "We had a row and he came after me, trying to talk to me. He didn't see the bus because he was looking at me. So yes, it was all my fault." She started to cry. "And now he's going to die because of me."

One of the paramedics looked up as he put a blanket over Philippe on the stretcher. "I don't think he's going to die, Mademoiselle. The doctor will examine him, but it looks like there's damage to his neck and concussion. He's very lucky. He didn't wear a seatbelt. Could have been worse." The man went back to helping his colleague load the stretcher into the ambulance.

Flora regained her ability to move and rushed forward to the ambulance. "Can I come with him to the hospital?"

"Are you his wife?"

"No. But we are...we were...I'm his—" She didn't quite know how to explain it.

"Fiancée?"

She nodded, not caring if she told a lie. "Yes. That's it."

The man nodded "*Ça va.*" He shot a look at the policeman. "Are you finished with this lady?"

The policeman looked up from his notes. "Yes, for the moment. Just give me your name and address and you can go."

Flora climbed into the ambulance and sat on a seat beside Philippe. She took his cold, floppy hand and held it to her cheek. She no longer cared about what he had or hadn't done. She couldn't even remember why she had flown into such a rage. It was unimportant and silly. He had to survive and walk away from this unhurt.

"Please forgive me, my darling," she whispered and closed her eyes. "Please God, let him get well and love me again. Holy Mary, please help us."

Philippe's eyelids suddenly fluttered. "Flora?" he whispered. "Are you there?"

She kissed his hand. "Yes, darling. It's me. I'm here."

"Don't go."

"I won't. I'll never leave you again."

He didn't reply but closed his eyes with a sigh. Flora held his hand all the way to the hospital, knowing she meant what she said. She would never leave him again. That other business, well, she would have to live with it or not have him, and that was too unbearable to contemplate.

***

Chantal walked up the street to the gallery, her heart sinking with every step. How hard it would be to face Gabriel. She had called him as soon as she arrived back at her apartment, and he was very happy to hear her voice. When he suggested they meet at the gallery so she could see the paintings, she was hesitant. Facing him again in private would be hard enough, but in public? That could be even harder. How would they hide their feelings for each other under the scrutiny of others? But Gabriel assured her only the gallery owner would be around at that time in the morning, so Chantal agreed. In any case, perhaps it would be better like this. At least they wouldn't be able to do anything of an intimate nature. She couldn't face the thought of having to reject him. Mulling these thoughts over in her mind, she opened the door to the gallery and stepped into the cool, quiet space.

She was immediately hit by the sight of the large canvases on the white walls just inside the entrance. Mesmerised, she stared at the images of The Bay of Angels in different lights. The paintings were breathtaking, dramatised by the shadowy figure of a woman in the foreground. Chantal knew it was her, yet not her: a woman, any woman standing at a window somewhere, dreaming, looking at the view or simply lost in her own thoughts. The last of the canvases, where the woman glanced over her shoulder at the spectator was the most powerful of all. The eyes were clearly hers, and at that moment, Chantal felt she was looking into her own soul.

A hand touched her shoulder, making her jump. "Chantal."

She turned slowly and met those arresting grey eyes. "Oh, Gabriel, the paintings are beautiful."

"I'm glad you like them," he said, not taking his hand off her shoulder. "I've sold quite a lot."

She pointed at the last painting. "This one too?"

"Not yet."

"Then I'd like to buy it."

"I'll give it to you."

"I'd prefer to pay for it." She moved away from his touch. Not because she didn't like to feel his hand there, but because she liked it too much.

"I won't let you." He paused for a moment. "How's your husband?"

She glanced at the woman sitting at a desk, typing on a laptop at the far side of the gallery, and then turned to face him. "Jean's getting better. He's in a clinic near Geneva for rehabilitation. He's been…it's been…strange."

Gabriel frowned. "What are you doing here? Why aren't you there, with him?"

"He sent me away. He said he wanted to be on his own for a while—to find his own way forward. He told me to come back here to sort out my own feelings and decide what course I should take on my own journey. And to find out how I feel about him…and you," she added.

"Brave man. Does he know about me? Did you tell him?"

Chantal shook her head. "No. I just said I had a liaison with someone else. But he seemed to know even before I said that. It's eerie the way he has some kind of second sight and can see right into my mind. I could never lie to him."

Gabriel looked across the gallery at the woman, who was now looking at them with undisguised interest. "We need to talk. Can we go somewhere for a drink? Or dinner? Or to my house? There's no one there tonight. We could—"

She stopped him by touching his chest, in a gesture that pushed him away but was meant to be pleading. "No, not there. A drink, yes. A glass of wine at the bistro by the harbour."

He nodded. "Yes. I'll meet you there in about ten minutes. I need to check something with the lady who owns the gallery first."

"I'll see you there." Chantal nodded at the woman and left the gallery. She walked the short distance to the bistro, where she quickly found a table by the window and ordered a glass of St Julien for them both—the very best Bordeaux they had enjoyed together on many occasions, especially after making love. Would they ever have those moments again?" Chantal knew the answer instinctively. Her thoughts were interrupted by the arrival of Gabriel, who, with an easy stride, entered the bistro and joined her at the table.

He picked up his glass and took a sip. "St Julien. Just like in the old days." He looked at her over the rim of his glass.

"That's the only thing that is." She kept her hands in her lap, twisting them, rubbing the sweat off them against her skirt. It was unbearable to sit with him like this, not touching or connecting in any way.

"Chantal?" he said gently. "You're not drinking your wine."

"I don't want it."

He put down his glass. "Are you not well?"

She looked out of the window at the boats in the harbour without really seeing them. "Me? I'm fine." She turned to look at him. "That's the first time in months anyone has actually asked how *I* am. I haven't even asked myself that question. I've been too busy worrying about Jean and trying to figure out what to do and how I'm going to carry on."

He groped under the table for her hand and squeezed it. "You must look after yourself too." He took a deep breath, cleared his throat. "Chantal, I know I shouldn't ask you this right now, but I can't wait. I need to know if you'd be willing to…to come and live with me? And to—eventually—marry me?"

She put her other hand over his, savouring the feel and warmth of his skin. It both calmed and excited her. She looked at his handsome face, so full of concern, his eyes so full of love. How easy it would be to simply say yes. Yes, I'll leave Jean now that he's well again. Yes, I'll walk away from a marriage of thirty years and a man who loves me. Yes, I'll forget the past and embrace the future. At that moment, Chantal wanted to do just that: leave everything behind and start a whole new life. It would have been wonderful and frightening but truly exciting. She pulled her hand away.

"Gabriel, I can't answer that right now, I just can't."

He let go of her hand and rested his on her knee, then ran it under her skirt, up her thigh. Their eyes locked. Chantal suddenly found it hard to breathe. She licked her lips. His hand travelled to her groin before she pulled back.

"Don't," she whispered. "Please don't touch me like that. It makes me so hot and confuses my thinking."

His eyes burned as he looked at her. "I want to confuse you. I want you in my bed."

She got up. "I have to go. Gabriel, I can't think right now. I know it's unfair but I have to ask you to wait."

He shot up and pulled her to him. "Don't say you don't want me."

She squirmed, aware the other guests in the bistro were staring at them openly. "I'd never say that," she whispered. "Of course I want you. But I can't give in to that right now. Give me a little time. Let me breathe and think. Give me the same space Jean did."

"I'm not him," Gabriel snapped and let her go so quickly she nearly fell. "I'm no saint. I couldn't do what he did. But maybe he doesn't love you as much as I do? Maybe he doesn't need you or want you as much in a physical sense? Have you ever thought of that?"

Chantal walked to the door. "I'll think about a lot of things. But now I'm going to take a break and let all of this rest for a while."

"Where are you going?"

"Back to work," Chantal said and left Gabriel and the bistro, banging the door shut behind her.

Chapter 18

There was a strange silence when Flora walked into the agency. Iris, wearing earphones, was typing into her computer, and Daisy was looking through the post that had just been delivered. They both looked up when Flora closed the door.

"Already at work?" Flora said. "And Daisy came in on time for a change? I'm impressed."

Iris tilted her head toward the inner office door and rolled her eyes. Daisy drew her finger across her throat and made a face.

"What's going on?" Flora asked, puzzled. Both Daisy and Iris looked sober and somewhat flattened.

Iris took off her earphones. "*She* is back," she hissed.

Flora stopped in her tracks. "Who? Oh God, not Chantal! It's too soon. We haven't sorted everything out yet. And the accounts are in a mess, and some of the outstanding fees haven't been paid. I was going to work on that, but then stuff happened and— "

"Yeah, like Ross's cover being blown," Daisy said under her breath. "He's a prisoner in his own home now, thanks to the bastard who took those pictures."

"And Philippe was in an accident on Friday and is still in hospital," Flora added.

"Oh no!" Daisy exclaimed. "Is he all right?"

Flora nodded. "Yes. He was lucky. Concussion, two

cracked ribs and a hairline fracture of a vertebra. He's being kept in until the end of the week for observation."

"Thank God for that," Daisy said. "How did it happen?"

"I don't want to talk about it right now," Flora said, looking at the door of the inner office. "I have to go in there and face the muzac, I suppose. I bet someone's in a right snot."

"She's not exactly dancing the cancan," Iris said drily. "And she said to send you in as soon as you arrived."

Flora's hear sank. She walked to the door. "Wish me luck."

"If we don't hear anything after half an hour, we'll send in the troops," Daisy promised. "Good luck and…" She lowered her voice. "Don't take any shit from you know who."

"I'll do my best." Like a condemned prisoner, Flora opened the door.

Chantal looked up from the computer screen. "Flora. Please come in and close the door."

"Hello, Chantal," Flora said, trying to keep her voice steady. "How's your husband?"

"Improving. Please sit down."

Flora sat down on the edge of a chair in front of the desk.

"I've been looking at accounts and sales."

"Yes?"

Chantal's eyes were colder than the Mont Blanc glacier. "They're very strange. Some of the properties have been sold for a lot less than was on the books. And I see here there are emails from some very unhappy sellers. Some of them have withdrawn their properties from us and gone to other agencies."

Flora twisted her hands in her lap. "Yes, well, it's all part of the new plan."

Chantal raised one eyebrow. "I don't remember us discussing a new plan. Would you care to enlighten me?"

Flora cleared her throat. "Well, you see, it was because of Dottie and Peter and how she loved this house that was nearly a wreck, but it was too expensive and they wouldn't afford to buy it *and* do the renovations. And then they passed on that one, which was a house that had been for sale for over four years, so I—"

"So you took it upon yourself to get the sellers to lower the price?"

Flora nodded.

"And the house was sold?"

"Yes." Flora plucked up her courage to continue. "This made me think that if we were *honest* about the houses we have for sale and didn't try to cover up cracks or damp or drainage problems and made the prices more realistic, we'd sell off all those wrecks that have been sitting there for years."

"And this is working?"

"Uh, yes. It's beginning to move a little. We've sold three houses that were just sitting there."

"Three. Well done." Chantal took off her glasses. "Look, Flora, I'm not happy with what you did at all. I appointed you as temporary manager because I trusted you. And then, as soon as my back's turned, you go and start changing the whole image of my agency. I find that both underhand and sneaky. You knew I was busy looking after my husband, and you took advantage of that. Not a very nice thing to do. You've probably ruined my business, and we'll never see good sales again."

Flora bristled. "I don't agree. I think you'll see that business is very good quite soon. Okay, so some of the sellers will pull their properties, but we'll see a lot more people who have old and wrecked houses come to us because we consistently sell off the ones that seem impossible to move, simply by being upfront about the state of the houses. We might even get together with builders and carpenters and other craftsmen and specialise in this kind of thing."

"I don't remember asking you to do this," Chantal snapped. "Why on earth did you feel you had to go and get all noble and honest? Not just because of Betty and Paul, was it?"

"Dotty and Peter," Flora corrected. "Not just because of them. But they were the catalyst, I suppose. I got so sick of lying to people, of having to cover over the cracks and shove bread in the oven so the smell of baking would cover the stink of mould and of telling people they'd get planning permission to extend or rebuild. And I just couldn't manage the mayor's office at all. They won't even talk to me because I'm not French." She drew breath.

"I distinctly remember you saying you had no scruples about telling a few lies when I interviewed you for the job. You actually told me you were good at lying."

"I lied."

Their eyes locked and Chantal's mouth quivered for a second. Then she regained her composure and the cold stare. "Well, I'm afraid the only option I have is to fire—" She stopped as the phone rang and picked it up.

"*Agence du Soleil*, Chantal Gardiner. *Bonjour* Madame. *Oui…*" Chantal frowned as she listened to the voice continue at the other end. "Oh, yes that's right," she said when there was a pause. "We're going in a new direction. We feel we should be more honest about the houses we sell. It's something I've been planning for a long time." She paused as the voice started again. "Unusual? Of course. But I prefer to think of the people who come here, often to start a new life, rather than trying to squeeze the last penny out of them like other agencies." There was a brief pause. Then Chantal said, "Thank you, Madame," and hung up. She turned to Flora. "Where was I?"

"You were going to fire me. I think."

Chantal blushed and cleared her throat. "Oh, yes, well… I'm reconsidering, following that call. It was from a woman who had just bought the old cottage outside Vence. It's been for sale for years. But she got it for a good price, she said, and nobody tried to cover up the flaws. And someone was very helpful and recommended a builder who has just agreed to do the work for a reasonable sum."

Flora nodded. "Yes. I've signed on some contractors who wanted to advertise on our website—builders, plumbers and even an electrician. All highly recommended by people who have restored old houses around here. The contractors will pay for the ads, of course. Some of them have already agreed to the annual fee. That's what I mean when I talked about builders and carpenters. They'll get a little picture on the sidebar of the homepage. And we might even set up a page for them once we get a few more. Plus, I think the wrecked cottages should have 'approved builder available' or something at the bottom of the descriptions."

Chantal squinted at the computer screen. "I don't see those payments here."

Flora got up and walked to the other side of the desk. "If you go to the previous page, you'll see them."

Chantal clicked her mouse. "Oh, yes, there they are. Hmm, that looks good. Not a bad idea."

"And I'm planning to get some interior designers to advertise, too. Well," she corrected herself, "you'll have to take care of that when I'm gone."

Chantal looked alarmed. "Gone? Where are you going?"

"You just fired me," Flora said, straightening up.

"Did I? In that case, you're hired again."

"If I take the job," Flora said.

They looked at each other.

Chantal burst out laughing. "You know, you're so very like someone I know."

"Who?"

"Me."

Flora couldn't help smiling. "Yeah, and you sometimes remind me of me when I was five."

Chantal sighed. "I haven't laughed like that for many weeks. It felt so good."

"I know. I haven't felt much like smiling the past couple of days."

"Why not? Something's' wrong?"

"Yes." Flora went to sit down on the chair again. "My...the man I'm..." She hesitated. How could she describe Philippe? Her lover? Her boyfriend?

"The current man in your life?" Chantal suggested. "He's left you?"

Flora's shoulders slumped. "No. He was in an accident and now he's in hospital." Tears welled up in her eyes. "And the accident was my fault."

"Oh, my dear, that sounds terrible. Is he badly injured?"

Flora shook her head, groping for a tissue in the pocket of her trousers. "No, but he could have been. He could be... dead."

Chantal walked around the desk and put her arm around Flora's shoulder. "There, now. It isn't so bad. Look, let's go to the café and have a big cup of café crème and a croissant and you can tell me all about it."

Flora nodded. "Sounds good to me."

They walked out through the front office together, meeting the astonished eyes of Daisy and Iris.

"Please look after things while we have our coffee break," Chantal ordered. "We'll be back in about an hour."

"This must be some kind of weird dream," Daisy muttered as they left.

Flora winked at Daisy over her shoulder, cheered by Chantal's sudden offer of friendship. It would be good to talk to someone. But once they were seated at a table in the small café and had ordered their coffee and croissants, she found it was going to be more about Chantal than her.

* * *

The coffee grew cold in their cups as Chantal poured her heart out to Flora.

"How terrible," Flora said when Chantal paused. "Your husband so confused and so lost. And you looking after him full-time. That must have been so hard."

Chantal nodded. "It was a difficult life. And Jean was so changed, so *gone*, as if the real person had left and been replaced by some kind of zombie. It was worse at the beginning when he used to have these violent temper tantrums. But then he was put on medication which calmed him, even if it did make him slower than ever."

"How come nobody detected the tumour then?"

"Wrong diagnosis. The doctors have asked for the records of the tests they did three years ago and they showed that they were wrongly assessed. And the brain scan was mixed up with another patient with a similar name. At the time, I just accepted what they told me. Jean's family history also indicated early dementia was something in his genes. So I just carried on, living with this shell of a man."

"It must have made you feel as if he had died. The real Jean, I mean," Flora said.

"Yes, exactly. And now, it feels as if he's back from the dead, and I don't know how to cope with that."

"Because you love someone else?"

Chantal stared at Flora. "How did you know?"

Flora shrugged. "I guessed. And…" She hesitated. "I've seen the paintings."

Chantal looked startled. "The paintings? You've been to the exhibition?"

"Yes. And I met the artist. Gorgeous man. I don't blame you for falling in love with him."

"He's very attractive," Chantal agreed. "And a wonderful lover."

Flora squirmed. It was enough of an adjustment that Chantal was being so friendly, but this kind of revelation was too personal. "It reminds me of that movie…*Le Retour de Martin Guerre*. I saw it on TV recently. The soldier who had been presumed dead in action comes back after ten years and his wife has remarried."

Chantal nodded. "It's beginning to feel like that." She stared into her cup and picked up the spoon, stirring the coffee absentmindedly. "And I don't know what to do."

"How do you feel about Gabriel?"

Chantal looked up with a dreamy expression in her eyes. "I'm so physically drawn to him that all I have to do is meet his eyes and I want to get into bed with him. He feels the same. But is that love? Or simply lust?"

"And…your husband? Jean?"

Chantal looked bleakly at Flora. "I'm not sure. We were just like that at the beginning. And all through our marriage we had a very physical relationship. But that was a long time ago. Of course I love him, in a way. But I don't know if I love him as a husband or just as this person who has been part of my life since I was in my early twenties. We had such a happy marriage, but then…during his illness, I began to hate him."

Flora nodded. "Understandable. And now that he's better?"

Chantal shrugged. "I'm not sure. He's different—more serious and thoughtful. But it's been so hard to adjust to the fact that he's getting back to normal. Harder for him, of course. He says he feels like Rip van Winkle. And now he sent me away and won't let me go back until he calls for me. He said he wants me to find myself or some such nonsense."

"Maybe he needs to get strong all by himself before he can ask you to go back to him?" Flora suggested, so swept away by Chantal's story she forgot her own. "He might feel he doesn't want to lean on you because then he'd feel less of a man."

"Yes, I think you're right. Jean was always so proud and

so independent. And he knows I've been with another man. He was very understanding. I found that difficult. I wish he weren't so saintly and noble. It makes me feel guilty."

"I'm sure that's not what he wanted," Flora soothed. "He's probably trying to get you to make up your own mind. You wouldn't want to live with him if he was needy and dependent, would you?"

"No. That would be the same thing all over again, except perhaps worse." Chantal sighed and pushed the cup away. "It's gone cold. Shall we order another one?"

Flora got up. "No. I think we should get back. We have lots of things to sort out, and I wanted to show you the changes I'm planning for the website."

Chantal nodded. "All right. Thank you for listening. But I'm afraid I was a little too preoccupied with my own problems to listen to yours."

Flora paid the bill. "Nothing much to talk about. I just have to work it out for myself."

"Is it a big problem?"

Flora sighed. "I'm beginning to think it is."

* * *

Chantal threw herself into work. The agency business was quite chaotic, as Flora had changed a lot of things, including the website. The properties for sale were no longer illustrated with glamorous photos of pristine houses and gardens. The new images were still lovely, but the tumbledown cottages hadn't been Photoshopped or cosmetically enhanced. Instead the potential of each property was emphasised, with the dilapidated houses photographed against the back drop of wonderful views or lovely, if overgrown, gardens. The possible rebuilding and extension of each house were also stressed but accompanied by a warning that the house in question needed a lot of work. The word 'updating', Chantal's description of choice, was never used to brush over a bad state of affairs.

It was a little frightening to see this huge change and to deal with disgruntled sellers who didn't feel they should accept a more realistic price for their badly built villas. But then she became more and more enchanted with the idea of specialising in selling wrecks with great possibilities. And wasn't it more exciting for buyers to get a house dirt cheap that they could turn into their dream house, rather than fooling them into buying a house that would turn into a horrible money pit? People from all over Europe were already beginning to contact them, and most of them wanted to put their own stamp on what they bought. They didn't seem to mind that a lot of the houses had to be practically rebuilt as long as they got it for a good price and could get a builder recommended by the agency. It was a whole new way of doing business nobody seemed to have thought of. It was exciting and challenging and just what Chantal needed. She nearly forgot about her personal life as she got more and more involved with turning the agency into something completely different. When Gabriel called a few days later, she found it difficult to pull herself away from her concerns about the new developments.

"I want to see you," he said. "We need to talk."

His voice was enough to make her face flush. "Yes," she said. "We do. But not—" she stopped herself before she said 'in bed'.

"We could walk on the beach, maybe?" he suggested, as if he had read her mind. Or maybe he felt the same? "Public and private at the same time."

"Which beach?"

"How about somewhere near St Tropez? A long drive for you, but I have my studio here now, and I'm busy with a commissioned painting. We could meet at Tahiti Beach. It's not crowded at this time of year. Please say you can come."

Tahiti Beach. Where they had spent so many long summer days, swimming, lying in the sun, having lunch at the little beach hut. Chantal closed her eyes and remembered his hands slowly applying suntan lotion on her hot skin. Was that really a good place to meet? But it was nearly October. Still warm but not hot enough to strip off. There would be people around but in the distance. It would be a long drive but it would allow her to think.

"Yes," she said. "I can."

* * *

Flora had to get used to being back in the outer office while Chantal reclaimed her position and her own inner sanctum. But the new deal of the agency gave the whole office a buzz, and they all worked together to project the new face and feel of the agency. This gave her less time to think and worry about Philippe. She rang the hospital every morning to ask about his recovery and was told that he still needed to rest and that he would be able to receive visitors 'soon'.

But the next time she called, she was told he had been released that morning and had gone home by taxi.

"Oh no!" Flora exclaimed. "He wasn't ready to leave. How's he going to manage on his own?"

She could nearly see the nurse's indifferent shrug. "That's not our problem. I'm sure he's fine or the doctors would have kept him in." She hung up without saying goodbye.

"Bitch," Flora said into the phone.

"Were you talking to me?" Iris enquired from her place beside Flora.

"No, that nurse. Said Philippe went home this morning. But it's too soon," Flora moaned. "How's he going cope all alone?"

"Why don't you go there and see if you can help him?" Daisy suggested. "It's nearly closing time anyway, and it's Friday, so the next hour or so will be quiet in here. Chantal took the afternoon off, and Iris and I can deal with any phone calls until we close up shop. Won't we, Iris?"

Iris shrugged. "I suppose." She checked her watch. "Coming up to five. Only an hour to closing."

"Nice watch," Daisy said. "Isn't that a Hermès tank watch?"

Iris looked suddenly uncomfortable. "Yes it is."

"Gorgeous," Daisy said.

"Thank you," Iris replied curtly.

"And I couldn't help notice the new handbag," Daisy continued. "That's the latest from Michael Kors, if I'm not mistaken. Have you won the lottery or something?"

"I came into a little money when my aunt died last July," Iris said. "Not that it's any of your business."

"Gee, gosh. Of course. Sorry," Daisy said and turned to her computer. "Well, let's get the last things done so we can get out of here, too."

Flora hovered at the door. "Uh, Iris…"

"Yes?" Iris snapped.

"Could I borrow your car? If you're not using it yourself, of course."

"My car?" Iris looked uncertain. "Where are you going?"

"Vence. To see Philippe."

Iris dug for the keys in her fancy handbag. "Okay."

"You still have that old car?" Daisy said. "Maybe now you can buy yourself a new one?

Iris frowned. "I might, but it's not—"

"Any of my damn business. I know," Daisy said and muttered "Shut up, Daisy" to herself as she resumed typing.

"Do you want me to drop the keys through your letter box?" Flora asked.

Iris nodded. "Yes, please."

"Great. Okay thanks for the loan of the car. I'll bring it back in one piece, I promise."

Flora walked out of the office, got into the car and drove off, leaving the traffic-choked streets behind and taking the road through the hills behind the coast. Up there, the road wound itself through thickets of cork oaks and umbrella pines in scary hairpin bends around huge boulders. The fresh air whipped her hair around her face, and the evening sun warmed her back. Flora felt a calm wash over her as she drove, and she switched on the car radio to listen to some music during the trip. On the classic channel, Marlene Dietrich sang 'Falling in Love Again' in her sultry voice, which made Flora feel both nostalgic and happy. Yes, they would be falling in love again, starting over with a new understanding. She just had to get over Philippe earning money from spying on celebrities. Or make him stop if she could.

She was so preoccupied with these thoughts that the drive seemed shorter than ever. Before she knew it, she had reached the gates to Philippe's house. Finding them open, she simply drove in and pulled up beside a small Citroen parked below the front steps.

Anxious to see Philippe, she switched off the engine and hurried out of the car and up the steps. The door was open, and she could hear voices from the living room. Flora stopped and listened. Philippe was talking to a woman. She peered in and could see him sitting on the sofa, smiling at someone coming out of the bedroom: a woman with short black hair, wearing only a skimpy towel.

"I'll just dry off and then we'll have dinner on the terrace," Flora could hear the woman say in French.

"*Oui, ma chère Sophie*," Philippe replied. "You're a very good nurse."

The woman giggled. "Only if you do what I say, *mon chou*."

Flora backed away from the door and started down the

steps again to the car. But Philippe had spotted her and caught up with her as she was getting back into the car.

He took her arm. "Flora? What are you doing here?"

"I came to see if I could do anything for you," she answered in a half-sob, shaking off his hand. "But I see you already have plenty of help."

"Oh, you mean Sophie? She's nice, but she's—"

"Yeah, I bet." Flora slammed the door shut in his face and started the engine. She blinked away tears, ignoring Philippe's protests as she raced down the drive and onto the main road.

Chapter 19

Chantal had plenty of opportunity to think during her drive to St Tropez. At that time in the afternoon, the traffic was already heavy. When it slowed to a crawl before the round-about to St Tropez, she cursed herself for having taken the busy coast road instead of going around Ramatuelle, which would have taken her directly to La Baie de Pampelonne and Tahiti beach. She would be stuck there for at least twenty minutes. When the traffic came to a complete stop, she rolled down the window and gazed out to sea, trying to block out the traffic noises. This was a respite before meeting Gabriel after an absence of over a week. The work at the agency had taken up all her mental energies, and she had pushed her personal problems to the back of her mind. But it all came rushing back as she sat there, looking at the glittering waves, the sailing boats returning and the seagulls swooping and dipping all around them. The sun was just above the tips of the mountains, and the pink hue of the clouds meant it was getting late, later than she had planned. Chantal picked up her phone and sent a text message to Gabriel, explaining she would be late. There was no reply. He was probably on his way and couldn't pick up his phone.

She switched on the radio and the voice of Jacques Brel singing *Ne Me Quittes Pas* filled the car. Chantal closed her eyes for a moment. *Ne Me Quittes Pas.* Don't leave me. That song again.

* * *

Flora heard her phone ping several times as she drove recklessly down the narrow road from Vence. She knew it was Philippe but didn't stop to check. She didn't want to hear his excuses. He was a liar and a cheat and he would never change.

She was nearly back in Antibes and stuck in front of a traffic light that had just turned red when she finally picked up her phone. No missed calls, just two text messages from Philippe. She gasped as she read the first one.

You silly girl, Sophie's my sister.

Flora clenched her jaw and mentally slapped herself. Of course! How stupid to jump to conclusions. But a pretty woman in a skimpy towel wandering out of a bedroom did look suspicious. She should have stayed and asked, of course, instead of running off in a jealous rage.

Flora was about turn the car around and drive back, but when she checked the second message, which said, *Flora, please believe me. I didn't take those photos,* she shook her head and told herself sternly to continue home. He might not have been a cheat but he was still a liar. Had he admitted to taking the pictures of Ross, she would have reconsidered. But now there was no way she could contemplate having any kind of relationship with him. Sad and bewildered, she drove back to Iris's apartment block. She parked the car, dropped the keys into Iris's post box in the entrance hall and walked down the hill to catch the bus home.

She had just reached her building when her phone rang. She checked the caller ID. Not Philippe but Ross.

"Hi Ross," she said. "How are things?"

"Strange," he replied. "Can you come here straightaway?"

"Here, where?"

"My house," he snapped. "You know I haven't been able to set foot outside my gates since the story broke."

"I know. Sorry. Been a little preoccupied with my own problems," Flora said, feeling guilty that she hadn't spared Ross a thought for a long while. He must have had terrible cabin fever by then. "I'll be over when I've had dinner."

"No," he urged. "I can't wait. Come over now. I'll order some food for us."

"What's the rush?" Flora asked.

"I got this very strange letter today. From the person who took those photos that broke the story about me."

"From Philippe?"

"No. From someone else."

* * *

"Read this before you do anything else," Ross said and handed her a letter.

Flora sat down on the Eames lounge chair in the living room and started to read.

Dear Ross,

First of all, I want you to know that I'm the person responsible for the revelation about your real identity. I took those two photos when you weren't looking and sent them to the press. I got money for it. Lots of money. I sold you for a lot more than thirty pieces of silver. But before you judge me, please read my reasons.

This is my story.

Two years ago, I gave birth to a little boy. He has huge brown eyes and his father's long eyelashes. He loves bread but hates strawberries. He hides the remote control for the TV and his plush doggie in the flap of his toy car and laughs when I find them. It sounds like champagne bubbles, if they had a sound.

I know nobody in the whole world who could make his grandmother laugh so loudly or cry in public. (My mother never shows any feelings whatsoever.) When my little boy is sad, tears the size of ping-pong balls roll down his cheeks and my heart breaks. When he's ill, he wants to sleep in my bed, his hot little body pressed against mine.

I don't know if you've ever had a baby go to sleep on your chest, listened to his breathing and realised how indescribably fragile that little body is and that you're the only person on this earth who can protect him from harm and make sure he grows up happy and healthy. I don't know if you've ever loved anyone so much it nearly gives you a heart attack thinking about it. His father died before knowing I was pregnant, and I feel so sad he isn't here to see our beautiful son.

But I digress. The fact that I'm a single mother struggling to pay the bills isn't the reason I did this to you. Two months ago, my little boy was diagnosed with a rare illness. The only cure is in America, at a clinic in New York, where they have only just started treating children with a new drug. This costs a lot of money, which I didn't have. My family isn't wealthy, and I knew no one who had the kind of money I needed. Then I heard the conversation at the restaurant after the art exhibition of how a photo of you—or the real you—could fetch a lot of money. I had my phone in my hand when I came back from the toilet, and I took a shot just to see how it would turn out. The photo was sharp enough to send on by email to France Soir and other newspapers. Then I remembered I had a photo of you at the beach, so I sent that one too. I got 20000 euros for each shot and a cut of the royalties should they go viral.

Of course, now you'll say I should simply have asked you for the money, but I was too proud to beg. I thought that, as nobody knows where you live, the excitement would die down in time. I'm sure it will when the vultures have found a new victim.

When you read this, I'll be on a plane bound for America

with my son. We'll stay there until he has been treated and is cured. My flat will be sub-let and my car sold by a friend who's helping out with the final details. I don't know if I'll ever return to Antibes. I only lived there to be close to my son's grandmother, but she passed away six months ago, so now there's nothing to keep me there. I'll probably go back to the UK and find a job there once my son is cured.

I wasn't going to tell you about all this, but then I felt that I didn't want anyone else to be blamed, which would further add to my guilt.

So now you know. I'm sorry if my actions have caused you a lot of problems. I hope the fuss will be minimal and that 'they' will never find your house.

Goodbye and good luck.

Iris

Flora sat with her hand over her mouth, staring at the letter. "Iris. It was Iris who did it. I can't believe it."

Ross took back the letter and folded it. "I know. I'm as shocked as you. Can't understand why she didn't just ask me for the money. I'd have given it to her like a shot."

"Of course," Flora said automatically, trying to come to terms with what she had read in the letter. "Poor Iris. How lonely she must have felt all this time. It explains her bad moods and why she looks so tired all the time. But why didn't she say anything? Daisy told me her story but she never talked about it to anyone."

"She's probably the kind who doesn't share her feelings with anyone and suffers in silence. They're the hardest to deal with."

"She must have been desperate. Otherwise she wouldn't have done it."

"No, I'm sure she wouldn't." Ross got up. "And now, here I am, dealing with the fallout. Shit, why didn't she come begging? I'd give anything not to be stuck behind high walls like this."

"You know what? If it wasn't her it would have been someone else," Flora remarked. "This was a disaster waiting to happen."

"Gee, you really know how to cheer a guy up."

"It's the truth." Only then did Flora notice that Ross had grown a beard. She suppressed a giggle. It made him look ridiculous.

He glared at her. "What's the matter? Is it the beard?"

Flora smirked. "Yeah, it's kind of funny looking."

He stroked his hairy chin. "Doesn't suit me, does it? But what else can I do?"

"I don't know." Flora got up from the chair. "Do you have any food? I'm starving."

"Not much, but I could order pizza or something."

"Yes, let's do that. I'll take the delivery so you won't have to show your beard, I mean face," Flora said and giggled again.

"I'm glad you find it so entertaining," Ross said glumly and picked up his phone from the table. "What kind of pizza do you want?"

"If they have something hot, I'll have that. I need to punish myself for being so stupid."

"I think there's one called Vesuvius," Ross said. "Will take the roof off your mouth."

"Perfect."

* * *

The traffic finally started to move again, and Chantal was forced out of her reverie. She hadn't thought much about the first time she met Jean, but the memories crowded into her mind as she drove through the streets of St Tropez, where she and Jean used to wander hand in hand looking for a romantic restaurant. Jean would be poking into the quaint little shops in search of a gift for her: a necklace made of colourful beads, a blue silk shirt to match her eyes or a book he knew she would love.

She had wandered there with Gabriel too, in much the same fashion nearly thirty years later. Two men in her life, who both loved her. It slowly dawned on her what had drawn her to Gabriel when they first met. He was so like Jean.

The parking lot beside Tahiti Beach was nearly deserted. Chantal parked under one of the bamboo awnings and walked across the boardwalk to the beach. Gabriel would be waiting for her at the little hut where they served wine and salad in the summer months and now, in the low season, coffee or herbal tea. They would close at the end of October.

The sun was low over the mountains and the dunes cast shadows across the beach. A chilly wind whipped at Chantal's hair. She took off her shoes, wrapped her cotton jacket tighter around her and walked barefoot across the cold sand toward the hut where she could see Gabriel's tall silhouette against the darkening sky. Shivering slightly, she breathed in the salty air and the smell of wood smoke from the stove in the hut. It would be good to sit in front of it with a cup of tea.

Glancing behind her, she thought she saw someone following her, but there was nobody there. Just her guilty mind playing tricks. But why guilty? Jean had told her to make up her own mind. He would accept whatever she chose to do. He had become so strong after his 'awakening', so independent. And distant, as if he was being pulled away from her by some mental process. Or perhaps it was a way of guarding himself from the sorrow that would come if she chose to leave him? Or maybe he didn't love her anymore?

"Jean," she said, looking up at Gabriel who had walked over to meet her. "I mean, Gabriel."

He took her shoulders and looked into her eyes. "You

have to make up your mind, my darling. It's either me…or him. You can't have us both."

She leaned her forehead against his chest and closed her eyes, breathing in his scent. "I know. And whatever I decide will hurt one of you."

"Have you made up your mind?"

She looked up at him and nodded. "Yes. I have."

Chapter 20

Once again, Flora drove to Philippe's house, this time in a rented car. It was Saturday morning and the agency was closed. She told Daisy Iris had left and where she had gone but not about her being the culprit in the Ross affair. She and Ross had agreed between them not to tell anyone.

"The story's out there now," Ross said. "Who was responsible is immaterial. In any case, if not her, someone else will be able to do the maths and link me to my real persona sooner or later. Iris has enough problems without being made look like a conniving, money-grabbing bitch."

Flora agreed, admiring his forgiving nature and compassionate attitude. Her mind turned to Philippe and her accusations without asking questions first. He had never lied to her or denied what he did. He had taken her criticism with great understanding and never pretended he was innocent or that it was an honourable thing.

"Sneaky and underhand, yes," he had said when they discussed it. "But if I stopped, all the others would keep doing it." This wasn't a great argument but probably very true.

Sweaty with nerves, Flora's hands slipped on the wheel as she approached the hill on which Philippe's house stood. She looked up at the beautiful villa towering over her. The gates were closed. She would have to press the call button on the intercom. Would he let her in? Not wanting to get out of her car, she picked up her phone and found his name in the contacts list. Her courage nearly deserting her, she decided to send him a text.

I'm outside the gates. I want to talk to you. Will you let me in?

She sat there and waited for a reply but got none. Then she saw the gates opening. Gathering up what little courage she had, she drove in and crawled up the hill while the gates slid shut behind her. No going back now. Her legs shaking, she got out of the car and started up the steps to the terrace. As she arrived at the top, she saw Philippe standing at the railing, looking at the view.

She joined him and gazed out across the hills and the blue sea in the distance. "Lovely day," she said.

He didn't move or look at her. "Yes."

"It's getting colder. And I think it might rain later."

"Probably."

Flora did her best not to get distracted by being so close to him, feeling the heat of his body and watching the wind ruffle his thick brown hair. She averted her eyes from the strong hands on the railing and sidled further away.

"I've come to say I'm sorry. I know now you didn't take those photos."

He turned slightly to glance at her. "You have proof?"

She nodded. "Yes. The person responsible has confessed. And when I learned who it was and what happened, I realised you would never do such a thing. That you've never lied to me and never would. It was wrong of me to suspect you." She drew a shaky breath.

"I'm glad you feel that way. But sad that you didn't trust me enough to believe me."

"I'm sorry about that." She put her hand on his arm. "Please say you forgive me and then I'll go."

"No." He caught her hand. "I don't want you to go." He turned to face her and the expression in his eyes made her heart leap. "Flora, you hurt me. And then the accident was the cause of your flouncing out of the house. I was desperate to catch you and to convince you I was innocent. Then the crash happened. I was lucky. It could have been a lot worse."

Flora started to cry. "Yes. You could have been killed and it would have been all my fault."

"And then you came here and saw Sophie and drew all the wrong conclusions because, again, you didn't trust me."

She lifted her tearstained face and glared at him. "Yeah, but hey, a naked woman coming out of your bedroom is kind of hard to see as something innocent."

"I can accept that. Especially on top of everything else you believed about me."

"Good."

"And I accept your apology."

Flora sniffed and wiped her eyes with the back of her hand. "Thank you."

He was quiet for such a long time Flora thought he was just expecting her to leave. She pulled away from his touch.

"I'll just go then."

He grabbed her shoulders. "No. Not until you've heard what I have to say. Will you listen to me?"

"Yes," Flora said, unnerved by the wild look in his eyes.

"Flora," he started, then took a deep breath and groaned. "*Merde*, I can't find the words to say how I feel." He shook her. "You're the most maddening woman I've ever met. The first woman I've ever wanted to slap, but at the same time I just want to throw you on the ground and screw you. A pretty brutal way to talk to the woman you love, but there it is." He looked up at the sky in desperation. "Dear Lord, what have I done to deserve this impossible girl?" He looked at her again. "I'm older than you. I've done and been involved in things you wouldn't like. You should run a thousand kilometres from me and find someone younger, nicer. Maybe some young man like that rich friend of yours, Ross or Joe or whatever his real name is."

Flora shook her head, her heart dancing, despite his tight grip digging into her shoulders. "I don't want anyone else."

"Prove it," he growled and pulled her so tight against him she couldn't breathe.

"How?" she mumbled into his chest.

"By marrying me."

She gasped and pulled back. "What? Did you just say—?"

"You heard. *Nom de Dieu*, say yes. I'm not going to ask you again."

"But I…I mean, I have to think—" She stopped. "Are you going to stop doing that celebrity stuff?"

"Not at the moment. Would that be a deal breaker?"

"You know I hate it. But…" She gave up. "Oh, what the hell. It's not as if you go around murdering people. I will marry you. Whenever, wherever, however you want."

"Probably the worst decision you ever made."

Flora laughed and threw her arms around him. "It probably is. But life's too short to be careful."

* * *

The sleet beat against the windscreen as Chantal drove up the avenue that led to the clinic. The weather had turned from bad to worse during the long drive up the mountain road, and she knew the rain would turn to snow further up. It was the start of the short, dreary late autumn, when everything turned brown before being covered in a blanket of snow. Winters and summers were lovely in the Alps. But autumn and early spring were dreary. She hoped Jean would be well enough to move out of the clinic and come home with her. He hadn't been in touch for two months, having made her promise to give him some space. But the time of separation was coming to a close, and he had called and asked her to come.

"We need to talk," he said, sounding calm and at peace. "I've been doing a lot of thinking and praying, and now I see a new road ahead."

Praying? What did that mean? Jean was a practising Catholic before he became ill but not in a fanatical way. Perhaps he had turned to prayer during this time of confusion? If only she could do the same. But her faith wasn't as strong as his. She knew there was a god or a superior being. She believed in some kind of spiritual existence in the next life, but her faith was sketchy and had no firm anchor in any one religion. How wonderful it would be to believe in prayer at that moment. To have something to turn to when life hit you and you had to make painful decisions.

She had left Gabriel at the beach after telling him she had to go back to Jean and that their many years together meant too much for her to break away from her marriage. Walking away from Gabriel broke her heart. But she couldn't choose a life with him and leave Jean, with whom she had spent most of her adult life. It was impossible to even consider abandoning a man who had suffered so much and then so bravely fought to get back to a normal life. Jean was part of the bigger picture, that of growing old together and supporting each other like so many married couples did. That was the best choice, the only choice for her. Loving Gabriel was a beautiful dream, and she would never forget their time together.

Glancing back as she neared the car park at the end of the beach, she saw Gabriel standing at the edge of the water with his hands over his face, bent over like an old man, his shoulders heaving. He was suffering and that was her fault. But he had initiated their love affair and knew the score. Not that it made it any less painful, but it diminished the guilt and blame.

Chantal found a space to park right in front of the main building of the clinic. She ran through the sleet and walked into the reception area and asked the young nun at the desk where she might find Jean.

"He's waiting for you in the sunroom," she said. "He just finished his retreat at the monastery."

Chantal took off her wet jacket. "Monastery? What monastery?"

"In La Clusaz, only half an hour's drive from here. It's a Carthusian monastery, an annex of the one in Chartreuse. Your husband asked to visit some time ago. He's spent a lot of time there. It has given him a lot of comfort and peace."

"Oh," Chantal said, bewildered. "I had no idea. He said something about prayer but…"

The nun smiled and nodded in the direction of the long corridor. "I'm sure he'll tell you all about it. It's the last door on the left."

Chantal's footsteps echoed in the dim corridor. She found the door, opened it and walked into a room so full of light she had to squint to see. She saw a tall silhouette at the big picture window and shaded her eyes with her hand. "Jean?"

He walked towards her. "Chantal. You're here at last."

She stood on tiptoe to kiss him on the cheek. "*Bonjour, mon amour.*" She stepped back to look at him. "You look wonderful," she said, realising on closer inspection that it was an understatement. He was the picture of health; his hair was glossy and back to its normal brown colour, his cheeks were pink and his eyes shone. Dressed in casual trousers and the blue cashmere polo neck she had sent him when she heard the weather had turned colder, he looked ten years younger than when she had left him at the end of the summer.

He smiled. "Thank you. I feel very well. But please, let's sit down over there by the window. It's bright there despite the bad weather."

Chantal walked to the group of easy chairs by the large picture window and sat down, looking out at the whirling snow. "The weather has turned very wintry. But it's better than the rain."

"Much prettier," he agreed and indicated a tray on the table in front of them. "I asked them to bring some tea."

"Wonderful." Chantal helped herself to tea. She sipped from the mug and nibbled on a *madeleine*, feeling a peace settle over her like a comforting blanket. It felt like coming home, finally settling into a comfortable relationship with the man she had loved since she was a young woman. Maybe they could rekindle that love and start afresh? That, and only that, would help her finally get over Gabriel. She looked at Jean. "So, when do you think you can get out of here? I can't wait to get you home and start our life again. I need your help with the agency, and I think we should look for a house somewhere. Something small with nice views and a garden."

He put down his mug and took her hand. "Chantal. I have something to tell you."

"What?" she said, bewildered by his serious tone. "If it's about the house, we needn't rush into anything, and if you don't feel like working for a while—"

"Slow down. It's not about that." He paused. "It's about me. About the rest of my life and what I want to do."

"And…?" she said with a feeling of doom.

He took a deep breath, and she noticed a light in his eyes that hadn't been there before. Something had changed him. Something big. "My darling," he started, "what I have to say will hurt you. But it will also set you free."

"What do you mean?" Chantal asked, feeling dizzy.

"I'm not coming back with you."

"You're not? But Jean…"

"Please, let me explain. I've spent these past two months doing a lot of thinking. And meditating and then praying. I just came back from a retreat in a monastery nearby. During that time, I had this experience, a calling, you might say. I knew then that I want to spend the rest of my life quietly and alone. Praying, doing God's work, away from the modern world and all the confusion. I feel it's my salvation and my destiny."

Chantal stared at him. He looked so serene and so determined. It was as if he had already left the real world and was travelling on some spiritual journey to the next life. "I don't know what to say."

He squeezed her hand. "Don't say anything. I know you love me in a way, but I also know you gave up something or someone who could make you happier than I could. I know you came here because you simply couldn't see any other way forward. That proves what an honest, kind, generous woman you are. I truly admire you for that. I'm not sure I could have done it, nor could I have looked after someone with dementia the way you did."

"I had no choice."

"Maybe. But now you do. I'm setting you free, Chantal."

"And yourself."

He nodded. "Yes. But aren't we all on our own journey? Don't we have to make choices only for ourselves sometimes? I came to a crossroads and through prayer found the right road. I think it will also help you find yours."

Chantal got to her feet and started to pace around the room. "It all sounds very tidy and neat, doesn't it? But I think you're being very selfish."

He nodded. "I suppose it would appear that way. But you came here to take me back, having made the sacrifice of giving up a relationship I have a feeling was very loving and happy. I'm not sure I could live with that kind of charity."

Chantal turned to him. "And I don't think I could live with some kind of…some kind of self-appointed saint!"

He nodded. "I can understand how you feel. But please, let's not part on a bad note. I'm leaving tomorrow to join the monastery. After that we won't communicate much. It's a closed order, and we're not supposed to have much contact with the outside world. You can write to me and I will reply. I suppose there are practical details that need to be sorted out—our legal separation and my turning all my worldly possessions over to you and my part of the agency."

Chantal stopped pacing. "Will I never see you again?" she whispered, suddenly struck by the inevitability of it all. She was being dismissed, rejected, sent away so he could enter this new phase of his life. She knew there was no stopping him and that he was right. There was no future for them.

"You can visit me at certain times of the year. If you want," he added, a touch of uncertainty in his voice.

She nodded. "Yes. I think I'd like to see you again. But perhaps not for a long time."

"No." He rose. "You should go. I'll sign all the papers for my release from the clinic. I'm sorry it's cost you so much money."

She shrugged. "What does money matter? You recovered. That's worth more than money."

"Yes. And you got your freedom. You may not see it like that right now, but in time you will."

"I'm not sure," Chantal mumbled, a dark cloak of sadness enveloping her.

"I am. I'll walk you to the door."

"Thank you." There was a finality in his voice that didn't invite arguments.

When they reached the entrance door, he kissed her on the forehead. "You will always be that beautiful young girl to me, with the bluest eyes and roses stuck in your dark hair. I'll never forget you, or the happy times. And we'll meet again, one day, in another life. Goodbye, Chantal. And thank you."

"For what?"

"For saving my life. And my soul."

Chantal walked slowly out of the clinic and got into her car. As she drove off in the gathering darkness and Jean's figure on the front step of the clinic became smaller and smaller, she felt a sudden lightness, a sense of letting go of something heavy. What a gift Jean had given her. Not only had he forgiven her and lifted the heavy burden of guilt from her shoulders, but he had also released her from the duty of caring for him. She could do what she wanted now, drive to Paris, or get on a flight to New York. Go on a cruise. Travel to the Far East. Whatever took her fancy. And Gabriel? Would he forgive her for making him suffer? Could they go back to the way they were? At that moment, Chantal didn't know if she wanted to. His love and the commitment he would expect was also a burden she wasn't sure she could carry.

With a sudden dart of excitement, she realised for the first time in her life she was truly her own person in charge of her own destiny. The thought gave her such a feeling of joy it made her dizzy. She took a deep breath, shook back her hair and laughed out loud. Freedom. It felt strange and frightening, but infinitely good. Jean and the long years of being his sole carer, Gabriel with his love and needs, even the problems with the agency disappeared in the slipstream of the car as she drove into the whirling snow to a new beginning.

Epilogue

The late spring sun shone through the windows of *l'Agence du Soleil*. Flora turned up the air conditioning. Being pregnant in hot weather was more than a little uncomfortable. The baby was due two weeks later, and then Flora would be on maternity leave. It would be nice to get a break. The past six months had been hectic. Their wedding had been a little rushed because Philippe had panicked when he found out about Flora's pregnancy. He didn't want his child to be born out of wedlock, he declared, when Flora said she wanted to wait until the baby was born. So they had a small wedding and a week's honeymoon in the cottage in Borme les Mimosas before they both had to get back to work; Flora at the agency, and Philippe on a photo shoot in the Alps for a big campaign. He had finally managed to get an agent who had soon been able to get him work with high profile advertising firms. Sneaking up on celebrities was no longer his bread and butter, to Flora's relief.

She shifted her large bulk in the chair and turned to the computer screen. There was an email from a buyer confirming their offer on a rundown villa in Cavalaire. The price was quite steep, despite its dilapidated state, but it was right on the waterfront with a private beach, so the location justified the price. Chantal would be pleased. She had worked hard at the agency all winter and the new ideas had matured into real prospects, with the agency beginning to be known as the only one to turn to for older houses that needed work and also for the excellent service in providing skilled workmen for building projects.

Daisy charged into the front office, interrupting Flora's thoughts. "Hey, it's like the North Pole in here. Turn down the air-co, willya?"

"Ah, come on, you know the hot weather's difficult for me," Flora pleaded. "Can't you put on a sweater or something?"

"I would if I'd brought one." Daisy rubbed her bare arms. "It's over thirty degrees out there. I'm not dressed for Siberia."

Flora turned down the air conditioning one notch. "Okay, I set it for twenty-two degrees. That's just over my comfort zone."

"It'll be a relief when that baby comes out. Have you got everything ready?"

Flora laughed. "Philippe's been working overtime to get the nursery decorated, and he's reading every baby-care handbook he can lay his hands on. I think he could get a master's degree in childcare by now."

"Older dads tend to be like that. It must be a shock to become a father at his age."

Flora flicked a rubber band at Daisy. "He's not that old… only forty-seven. He'll cope very well with fatherhood."

"I'm sure." Daisy shivered. "Even twenty-two degrees seems cold after the heat out there. But I'm sure the new girl will feel right at home."

"Oh, yes, she's starting today. I wonder what she's like?"

"Shh, she's coming in," Daisy whispered and nodded at the door that was opening to let in a tall young woman with shoulder-length dark-blonde hair and long slim legs that seemed to end at her armpits. A pair of glasses sat on her nose, and she peered through them with eyes of the darkest deepest blue.

"Hello," she said with an attractive lilt in her voice. "I'm here for an interview with Madame…Gardinier."

"Hi and welcome," Daisy said. "I hope your name isn't Violet or Rose."

"Or Petunia," Flora suggested.

"I'm sorry?" The girl looked at Flora with a mixture of annoyance and confusion.

"Just a little joke between the two of us," Daisy said.

"My name's Marika," the girl said and pushed the glasses further up her perfect nose. "And I'm from Sweden."

"Yeah, thought so," Daisy said. "Explains your plain looks and squat body."

Marika giggled. "I bet you're American. From Brooklyn, if I'm not mistaken."

"And you're a genius," Daisy declared. "Far too clever for this place. How did you guess where I'm from?"

Marika shrugged. "Easy. I lived in New York City for two years and shared a flat with a girl from Brooklyn. Nice girl. Great fun." She looked around. "So where's Madame what's-her-name?"

Flora looked at her watch. "She should be here. It's nine thirty. She must have known you were coming in."

Marika nodded. "Yes, we made the arrangement when I sent in my CV, or résumé as they say in America. She told me she'd be here on time."

"That's strange," Daisy remarked. "It's not like Chantal to be late. She's been working so hard all winter with the website and our new branch that recommends workmen and designers for all the houses being done up."

"I've just remembered," Flora exclaimed. "She's moving into her new apartment today. The renovations are finally done, so she said she was going to move in when the paint was dry. I don't think she wanted to wait one second longer than necessary. She told me we could hire the new girl if we liked the look of her."

Daisy nodded and looked Marika up and down. "And we do like the look of her. You're hired."

"Just like that?" Marika chortled. "Easiest job interview ever."

"Well, we're psychic," Daisy said. "But where are my manners?" She held out her hand to Marika. "Hi, I'm Daisy and the blimp over there is Flora. She's eleven months pregnant, so she can't get up."

Marika shook Daisy's hand. "Hi. Nice to meet you. I've heard about this agency. Saw the ad in a newspaper in Stockholm. I liked the look of it, and as I wanted a break for a year or two, I thought I'd apply for the job."

"What did you do before you came here?" Flora asked when she had shaken hands with Marika

"I'm a nurse. I love nursing, but I've had some health issues myself, so I took a year off to do something else."

"This will be far removed from nursing," Daisy said. "Except some of the houses are in need of intensive care."

"Not to mention the kiss of life," Flora quipped.

Marika laughed. "I think I'll like working here."

Flora switched off her computer. "Well, it'll be you and Daisy until I get back on my feet. And Chantal, of course."

"What's she like?" Marika asked.

Daisy looked at Flora. "Chantal? Well, a year ago I would have said she was a total bitch. But today…"

"She's a sweetheart," Flora said. "Best boss ever. We've been through a lot but now we're really cruising. But I warn you, she takes no prisoners."

"And she doesn't like anyone telling lies," Daisy said. She winked. "Right, Flora?"

Flora winked back. "You bet. No lying. Working here is quite easy. You just have to be good at one thing."

"What's that?" Marika asked, looking worried.

"Selling dreams," Daisy said.

* * *

The apartment was on the top floor of an old building overlooking the harbour. From her balcony, Chantal could see far out into the bay and the islands beyond. Leaning on the railing, she sipped her coffee and enjoyed the view, and the hot sun. Her home: her own space, her sanctuary. She turned and looked through the double doors into the living room, where furniture and boxes were piled on the polished floorboards. What a mess. But it would soon be sorted out: the sofa and chairs in front of the window, the bookcase at the far wall and her paintings hung where they would look their best. And Gabriel's two landscapes would hang in her new bedroom, so she could see them when she woke up.

She hadn't seen him all winter, even though the news of her separation from Jean was quite public. But his silence allowed her to find her way and to decide what she wanted to do next. She missed him desperately but couldn't face the idea of begging him to forgive her. If he wanted to forget her and move on, so be it. He had the right to make that decision without her clouding the issue with messages or phone calls. Apart from the pain in her heart, life was good.

After returning from her final visit to Jean, she threw herself into her work and, with the help of Flora and Daisy, turned the agency into one of the most popular ones among ex pats looking for old houses to restore all over Provence. Their sister site that vetted and recommended contractors had also taken off and everything now ran very smoothly. Flora and Daisy. Those two girls were true gems. They had both been made partners in the firm when Jean turned it all over to Chantal, and it was comforting to watch them shoulder the burden of marketing, accounting and website design. They were younger and more clued up when it came to internet marketing, too.

She turned her mind away from the agency and gazed again at the view of the harbour, where the marina was beginning to get busy after the winter. Sailing boats and motor launches were moored side by side, and the quay was busy with boat owners preparing for trips out to sea. This apartment was close to the popular restaurant and shops, something Chantal welcomed after the quiet of living in the hills. Being close to people was a good thing. She could sit here and watch the crowds and feel part of it all. She could even dine in one of the small restaurants each evening and chat to other guests and restaurant owners, the way one did in this friendly part of town. Alone but not lonely. And maybe, one day, she would meet someone…

Her eyes focused on a figure walking along the street leading from the harbour to her building. A tall thin man with floppy brown hair that he kept brushing out of his eyes. She knew that gesture so well, the set of the shoulders and that easy stride. Was it…? Could it be…? She turned away, didn't dare look. Maybe it was just a figment of her imagination? She looked again as the man drew closer. Yes. It was him. Gabriel. Walking toward her building. He looked up, saw her and stopped. Time stood still for a few seconds as they looked at each other.

Then he waved and shouted. "Chantal! I found you! May I come up?"

She hesitated. Then waved back. "Yes," she called. "Please do."

Moments later, the doorbell rang. Her heart pounding, she opened the door.

THE END

About the author

Susanne O'Leary is the bestselling author of more than twenty novels, mainly in the romantic fiction genre. She has also written four crime novels and two in the historical fiction genre. She has been the wife of a diplomat (still is), a fitness teacher and a translator. She now writes full-time from either of two locations; a rambling house in County Tipperary, Ireland or a little cottage overlooking the Atlantic in Dingle, County Kerry. When she is not scaling the mountains of said counties, keeping fit in the local gym, or doing yoga, she keeps writing, producing a book every six months.

Find out more about Susanne and her books on her website: http://www.susannne-oleary.co.uk

Made in the USA
Middletown, DE
18 February 2023